That Monroe Girl

by

Ilona Fridl

This is a work of fiction. Names, characters, places, and incidents are either the product of the author's imagination or are used fictitiously, and any resemblance to actual persons living or dead, business establishments, events, or locales, is entirely coincidental.

That Monroe Girl

Cover Art by *Rae Monet, Inc. Design*

The Wild Rose Press, Inc.
PO Box 708
Adams Basin, NY 14410-0708
Visit us at www.thewildrosepress.com

Publishing History
First Cactus Rose Edition, 2016
Print ISBN 978-1-5092-0461-8
Digital ISBN 978-1-5092-0462-5

Published in the United States of America

Dedication

I lost two dear women during the writing of this book.
One was my mother,
who was also Catherine from Virginia.
She was my biggest cheerleader
and bought my books to give to the family.
The other, Rona, I never met face to face,
but I wrote to her in England for over fifty years.
I lovingly dedicate this book
in memory of these two amazing women.

Chapter 1

Tombstone, Arizona Territory, 1883

Now Cat knew how a piece of laundry felt after it had gone through a particularly rough agitation. However, instead of being clean, she was covered with dust and fine sand that lined her traveling clothes and stuck to the sweat on her exposed skin. The desert wind blew in the stagecoach windows, carrying with it everything kicked up by the horses. She glanced at her maid and companion, Edna, wondering if she looked as haggard. Edna's thin face seemed older than her thirty-five years, and her black hair showed some gray streaks. Cat wiped her own face with a handkerchief that turned brown with the dirt.

The torture chamber halted with a jingling of harnesses, clatter of hoofs, and a groaning of the stagecoach itself. Cat's sides hurt, and her head began to throb.

"Tombstone!" shouted the driver. "We'll stop here two hours for supper at the hotel, then be ready to go again."

The elderly Mr. Carson, who occupied the coach with them, rose and opened the door. "Allow me to assist you, ladies."

The vehicle shook and bounced as the younger men on top climbed down. Mr. Carson held out his hand. Cat grasped it and stepped down in a cascade of dirt.

She shaded her eyes and called to the driver, "This is where we get off. Could you let down our trunks for us?"

His shotgun rider grabbed the rope hanging from a pulley on the porch roof of the hotel, connected its iron hook to the bindings on their hinged boxes. and lowered them to the wooden sidewalk by the hotel entrance. The driver tipped his hat to her, then removed his foot from the brake and guided the team to the back of the building.

Cat approached Edna, who sat on her wooden steamer trunk with a less than pleased expression. "You mean we have to carry these into the hotel?" Edna groused.

Cat put her hands on her hips. "This place is certainly less civilized than back east." She clamped onto the leather strap on one end of her own trunk and jostled it up the step into the entrance. "Come on. If I can do it, so can you."

As Edna tugged on her steamer, Cat glanced around the lobby. She marveled at the carpeted grand staircase with its polished black walnut banister and wondered how on earth they were going to get their belongings up to their rooms.

At her right, a large reception desk echoed the wood trim, and from behind it a slight, bespectacled man watched them. Cat set the end of her trunk down and stepped to the desk. "Sir, we would like a room in this hotel."

He adjusted his glasses. "Have you made arrangements in advance?"

Cat shook her head. "We've never been here before, but this is where the stage let us off."

"Is it just you two ladies? No escorts?"

She gave him an icy stare. "I have no husband, and my father is— Well, that is none of your affair. Do you want to rent us a room, or do I look elsewhere?"

"All right. But you both have to sign." He rang a desk bell twice, and two men showed up. "Take the ladies' trunks to Room Ten."

Cat motioned to Edna to join her, and while the burly men hoisted the heavy steamers up the stairs, the women signed the register.

"How long do you plan to stay?" the little man asked as he checked the book. "Miss Catherine Monroe and Miss Edna Harper. Is that right?"

"Yes. We don't know how long a stay, as yet. May I pay for a week?" She opened her reticule.

"Our weekly rate is ten fifty."

Cat counted out the coins, and he handed her the key. "I'll let you know in advance if we need the room longer."

"Thank you, ma'am. The dining room starts serving at six in the morning, eleven-thirty for the noon meal, and six in the evening."

Cat acknowledged the information, then followed the men up the stairs to Number Ten. She gave each of the men a quarter, and they nodded their thanks.

After the men left, Cat removed her gloves and poured some water from the flower-painted pitcher into the matching porcelain basin on the washstand. "I have to clean up before we go to supper."

Edna busied herself by undoing the buttons on Cat's traveling dress. "Miss Catherine, this is the eleventh town we've stopped in to search. When are we going to get out of this godforsaken part of the country and go home?"

Cat let her dress fall to the floor in a swirl of dust. "We have no home."

"I'm sure Ben would have let you stay at the house."

Cat sighed. "Now that Aunt and Uncle have passed, he didn't want to have me there. I could tell."

"How do you know your father will? Anyway, you don't remember what he looks like, and you don't have a picture."

"I have to find out. He would know about the family. And Cochise County has two Monroes listed." Cat finished unpinning her hair and let it cascade down her back. "Help me get the dirt out." She dug into her trunk and pulled out her hog bristle brush.

Edna took the brush as Cat sat on the chair at the writing desk. With Cat's tresses laid over the back of the chair, her companion started brushing. "What if he doesn't want you? What will you do then?"

"Then, my dear Edna, I will either have to marry a rich man or find work. I still have enough of my inheritance to last for a while." She gave an impish smile. "Don't worry. You'll still get paid every week."

Edna handed the brush back to her. "Hmm. I hope so. You owe me a raise in pay for dragging me out here."

Cat laughed and washed off at the basin. After she dried, she swiped the towel over her camisole and petticoats. "That sand went right through everything. We'll have to find a laundry this week." She drew her green silk dinner dress from the trunk and shook out the wrinkles. Edna helped her into it, and while Cat piled her hair up again, Edna washed and dressed. After they had wiped their shoes with a cloth, they went down to supper.

The host seated them in an elegant carpeted dining room, resplendent with three glittering chandeliers casting a creamy glow. Fine china, cut glass, and silver cutlery added to the atmosphere. A waiter came to them with menus. "Good evening, ladies. May I offer some tea or coffee while you decide what you want?"

They both requested tea and perused the board listing the special bill of fare for the day. When the waiter returned with their tea and lemons, the ladies told him they had decided on the Beef Wellington, and he left them. Cat poured some of the tea into her china cup and added sugar and lemon. She stirred and set the spoon on the saucer with a clink. "Lovely place, for a frontier town."

Edna made a face. "Not bad. However, I saw many saloons on the way in. That usually encourages rowdies."

"It certainly does," came a voice from behind them.

Cat turned and regarded a handsome young man with dark sparkling eyes. His blue-gray suit, clean starched collar, and dark blue vest with a watch chain drawn across it proclaimed him to be a gentleman of some sort, certainly not a "rowdy" or a cowboy. "Do you make it a habit of eavesdropping on people?"

He grinned. "In a way." He held out his hand. "I'm Jake Spencer, reporter for the *Tombstone Epitaph*."

She shook it. "Epitaph?"

"Newspaper. I was checking the new arrivals in

town. May I sit down?" He pulled a small notepad and pencil out of his jacket pocket.

Cat was mildly amused and curious. "Please. I'm Catherine Monroe, and this is my traveling companion, Edna Harper." Edna gave him a curt nod and raised an eyebrow in Cat's direction with a "would your uncle approve" look.

His face registered surprise and concern. "Monroe?"

"Yes. Is there something wrong?"

The smile immediately came back. "No—nothing wrong. How long are you going to stay here?"

"I don't know. Perhaps a week or so."

"Are you here to visit anyone special? It's odd to see two ladies traveling alone."

"No." Cat was feeling slightly uncomfortable. "Your questions are verging on personal."

"Not at all. We ask all visitors this." He raised an eyebrow. "Your answers could be deemed suspicious."

Cat puffed up. "It's really none of your or your newspaper's business why we're here."

"Then I take it this isn't a leisurely excursion of the West. You're obviously from the South."

Cat had had enough of his prying. "Yes, we are." The waiter was on his way with their food. "It was lovely to meet you, Mr. Spencer, but our meal is here."

He rose and gave a slight bow. "I see. I hope you ladies have a pleasant stay. Miss *Monroe*. Miss Harper." He pocketed his notepad and pencil and left.

Edna was quiet until the waiter finished serving and had left them alone again. "We've been to seven towns so far, and this was the first with a nosy newsman prying into our affairs. Usually they get the information from the registers."

Cat paused. "You're right. I wonder why he was so curious?" She shrugged. "We may never know now."

Edna shook her head. "I wouldn't be so sure about that."

Cat dug into her dinner, but a thought was nagging in the back of her head. What was the problem when she told him her name? She saw that expression. Did he know something?

****

The sky turned the gray-blue of twilight as Jake darted between buildings to the back of the Bird Cage Theater. Dara Foxwood was one of the main attractions and probably the biggest moneymaker. If anyone knew much about the Monroes, Dara would. Daniel had been a regular customer of hers for a year. It was still an hour before show time, and she should be in her room. He picked up a few small pebbles from the dirt and threw them against her window on the second floor.

The sash flew up and Dara stuck her head out. "Who's there?"

"It's Jake. Can you come down to the alley for a few minutes?"

"Sure. I'll be right down." She pulled back in and the window closed. Soon the stage door opened and she was there in her dressing robe. "What brings you here? Are you on a story?" The glow of the lamps from inside wasn't enough to hide the heavy makeup she wore. Jake always thought she would be a beautiful woman without all that grease and powder. As it was, she was invaluable as a source when he needed information. Men's mouths tended to loosen with drink and women.

"How much do you know about the Monroes?"

"Just what everyone does. Daniel works at Good Enough Mine, and his father and his brother John own the ranch at Sugar Springs. Why?"

"Have they ever mentioned a Catherine Monroe?"

"Never heard the name."

"She came in on the stage today with a traveling companion, Edna Harper. I wondered if there was any connection."

"You should know about the Monroes. Your father is Old Man Callahan's foreman."

Jake shuffled his feet. "Well, with the bad blood between the families, I didn't know them socially."

She gave him a mischievous smile. "Tell me, Jake, why are you so interested? Is she pretty?"

He paused. "As a matter of fact, she is. But I like a mystery when it gets thrown in my lap." He turned to go. "If you see Daniel, could you ask him about Catherine?"

She waved. "For you, my darling, I will."

Jake hoofed his way back to the newspaper office. Harvey Wilson, the editor-in-chief, scowled at him. "Again you come in just under the wire. You know we have to set the type for tomorrow's edition."

"I'll help you. I got sidelined again. Could be an interesting story." Most of the type had been set in neat columns on the plate. Jake gave the typesetter his notes to fill in another column. Small letter blocks started to fly into neat sentences.

Harvey slapped Jake on the shoulder. "What did you come across?"

Jake told him about Catherine.

Harvey stroked his mustache. "Monroe, huh? There could be a story there and maybe not. See what you can find out."

Jake took off his coat and rolled up his shirtsleeves halfway to his elbows, then slid sleeve guards over his arms. Setting the finished plate on the press, he started to ink it while Harvey set up the roll of paper. *I'll check on the beguiling Miss Monroe in the morning.* He was looking forward to this assignment.

Chapter 2

After breakfast, Cat finished loading the dirty clothes into a bag the hotel provided. "The man from the laundry is supposed to come and pick it up sometime this morning. I'll go to the courthouse by myself to look through the records."

Edna pursed her lips. "Do you think you should go around this town alone?"

Cat shook her head. "Please, I'm a grown woman. And if it's trouble you're worried about, I've got my derringer in my reticule. Remember, Ben taught me how to use it." She snapped on her gloves and grabbed her parasol. "I'll be back before noon, I'm sure."

"Be careful, Miss Catherine."

"I will." And with that assurance, she hurried to the lobby. To the man at the desk, she asked, "How do I get to the courthouse?"

He moved his glasses down. "It's on the southeast corner of Third and Toughnut Street. Just a block south of here."

"Thank you, sir." She left the hotel and opened her parasol. The sun was warming after what had been a cool night. August nights were quite different from those in Virginia. At least the brutal heat of day didn't continue when the sun went down.

Cat's shoes made a steady tap-tap on the wooden sidewalks. The hot dust in the street had its own odor as it blended with equine scents and leather. She raised her perfumed handkerchief to her nose to keep from breathing in dust carried on the warm breeze.

Arriving at Toughnut, she turned east and saw the newly built two-story courthouse with its fancy white brick trim and cupola on top. A covered entrance led into the reception area, where a clerk sat at a desk on one side. He looked up as she came in. "May I help you, ma'am?"

She closed her parasol and put it in the crook of her arm. "Yes. Could you tell me where the records department is?"

Following the clerk's directions, she made her way to a door at the far end of the building, took a deep breath, and walked in. A man was busily rifling through a file cabinet, and she cleared her throat.

He turned. "Yes, ma'am?"

Cat smiled. "May I see the tax rolls for Cochise County?"

He paused. "Why do you want to see that?"

"I'm searching for a person."

Nodding, he pulled a ledger off a shelf. "Here's last year's. You may sit at that table."

Cat thanked him and settled down to peruse the names. She was onto the second page when she felt someone was watching her. Glancing up, she recognized the darkly handsome reporter she'd met last night. He held his hat to his chest and gave her a bow. "Miss Monroe, what a pleasure to see you again."

"Mr. Spencer, you're not following me for some reason, are you?"

"Oh, no. I would never do that. I was doing some research on a story for the newspaper."

"Of course. I apologize. Good day."

He hesitated. "May I ask you something?"

Cat drummed her fingers on the ledger. "What is it?"

"Do you happen to be related to the Monroes at Sugar Springs?"

Her heart pounded in her chest. "You know a family named Monroe? What's his Christian name?"

"Albert."

She let out a cry and jumped to her feet. "You know Albert Monroe?" Then she burst into tears. "Oh, my…my prayers have…been answered!" She pulled out her handkerchief.

Jake sat her down again until she collected herself. "What's this all about?"

She sniffed. "You don't know how long I've been looking for him. Could you tell me where he is?"

"I'll do better than that. I can take you to his ranch. When do you want to go?"

"As soon as I can." She rose to gather her things.

"Whoa, Nellie! The ranch is forty-five minutes from here. I have to arrange transportation. Do you ride? Or do I need to hire a carriage?"

"Horses are fine. I'll have to change into riding clothes."

"I'll meet you with the horses at the hotel in an hour. Will that give you enough time?"

She hurried to the door. "Yes. And thank you!" Her feet flew on the way back to the hotel. *I've found him at last!* Still, a tinge of fear underlay her excitement. She didn't remember what her father looked like—she'd been just over a year old when he left. *How will I know it's him?*

Edna jumped as Cat burst through the door and grabbed onto her, swinging her around. "Edna, there's an Albert Monroe who owns a ranch around here. I'm going to see him!"

Edna pulled back and picked up the dress she had dropped. "How are you going to find him?"

Cat told her what had happened at the courthouse. "Mr. Spencer will be here within the hour."

Edna eyed her critically. "Miss Catherine, you're going unchaperoned with a man you barely know? He could be leading you out to take advantage of you."

"I have to trust him. This is the first bit of good news I've had on this whole quest. Anyway, I still have my gun with me." Cat found and dragged out her riding clothes. Working her way out of her dress, bustle, and petticoats, she slipped on the split skirt and white cotton shirt. Shrugging into a light linen jacket, she motioned to Edna. "Help me braid my hair."

Edna sat her on a chair and proceeded to remove hairpins. Brushing out Cat's tresses, she held a ribbon between her teeth, and after the plaiting was finished, the ribbon held the work together. Cat unbuttoned her shoes and found her riding boots, which she pulled on.

As Cat put on her broad-brimmed hat with a veil, she heard a knock and opened the door to a servant who spoke briefly. She replied, "Mr. Spencer is here? Tell him I'll be right down." She closed the door, slipped on her leather gloves, and transferred her gun from her reticule to a hidden pocket in her split skirt. "Don't worry about me. I can take care of myself."

Edna studied something on the floor. "Be careful anyway."

Cat met Jake outside holding two saddled horses.

He handed her the reins of a chestnut mare. "This is my sister's horse, Mazie."

She scratched the animal's nose. "Does your sister mind?"

"Peggy is in San Francisco visiting our aunt. I don't think she'd mind." He stood next to the saddle. "Need a leg up?"

Cat gathered up the reins and stood next to him. "Thank you."

He gave her a boost, then mounted his black-and-white pinto, and she noticed he had strapped on his gun and holster. He untied one of two canteens he had on his saddle horn and gave it to her. "Ready, Miss Monroe?" With her nod, they started out of town.

For a long time, there was just the sound of hoofs clomping in the soft dirt and the squeak of leather. Jake pushed the brim of his hat up and glanced at her. "What is Albert Monroe to you?"

She sighed. "I believe he is my father."

"Don't you know?"

She shook her head. "He left when I was just over a year old. I don't have a picture of him, and I don't remember what he looks like. So I'll have to trust his memory of his time back east."

"Where's your mother?"

She hesitated over telling him all this information, but he had been so nice, offering to take her to the ranch and supplying the horses, she relented. "She died a few months after I was born."

"And your father left after that?"

"Yes. He took my two brothers—"

"You say you have two brothers?" he interrupted.

Cat nodded. "John and Daniel."

"I went to school with them."

Something like a deep sadness welled in her heart. "You were friends with them?"

"I knew them. We weren't close. Then he definitely is your father. But why didn't he take you, too?"

"My aunt forbade it. She said the West was no place to raise a girl. So she and my uncle became my guardians."

"Where did you live?"

"In Alexandria, Virginia. My father was a Confederate soldier, but my uncle had moved his money to a northern bank, because he was convinced the federals would win. From what I was told, my father wouldn't live in Virginia after it was restored to the Union, so he moved his family west."

"Your aunt and uncle agreed to let you come out here on your own?"

Cat sighed. "They've both passed on. My eldest cousin, Ben, owns the house now, and I didn't feel I was welcome to stay. That's why I came in search of my father. How about you? Were you born in Tombstone?"

He laughed. "I'm older than Tombstone. It was founded six years ago after a silver strike. I was born on the Bar Seven ranch, which is near your father's. I'm the son of the ranch foreman and the cook, but, as soon as I came of age, I became a newspaper reporter. I like living in town better."

She shook her head in amazement. "For only being a few years old, there's sure a lot of people living there."

"Money ore tends to draw crowds. On top of that, the downtown has burned up twice, and we had that big to-do between the Earps and the Clantons a couple years back. That got us a bad reputation for being a lawless place, but we're no worse than anywhere else, in my opinion."

Cat enjoyed their conversation, and the time flew. Soon they were in sight of the Sugar Springs Ranch. Acres of wooden fence wound around, leading to a series of hills. By the road, a gate with a sign over it announced the ranch, and beyond it a gravel path led to the first hill, where it disappeared into the trees.

Jake stopped his horse in front of the gate. "Well, Miss Monroe, here we are. Do you want me to come with you?"

"Please do. And call me Cat."

"Thank you. You can call me Jake, if you'd like."

She hesitated, then drew in a breath. "I'm nervous, but I've come so far, I have to do this." She lightly kicked Mazie's side, and the horse trotted in, with Jake riding his steed behind. In what seemed like no time a cloud of dust rose behind the trees, and a man on a horse came galloping toward them.

"Uh-oh, maybe coming in with you wasn't such a good idea," Jake remarked. Cat wondered what he meant. They both pulled up their horses as the rider closed in and yanked his rifle out of the saddle holster.

"What's the meaning of this? Jake, you have grit, coming on Monroe land." He aimed the rifle at Jake.

Cat shook off her shock. "Mister, he escorted me here. I'm looking for Mr. Monroe."

The man spit in the dirt. "Yeah, and who are you?"

"My name is Catherine Monroe."

The man stared at her, then turned to Jake. "What the hell is the meaning of this?"

Jake calmly said, "This lady came into town yesterday searching for her father. She was raised out east and says her father left with her two brothers long ago to come west. She believes that Albert Monroe is he." Jake waved his hand toward the man. "Cat, this is Ned Hadley, the ranch foreman."

Ned angrily waved his rifle at both. "What kind of cock-and-bull story are you concocting? Did Callahan put you up to this?"

"I haven't been to the Bar Seven in over six months."

Cat steamed. This Ned seemed to act like she wasn't there. "*Mr. Hadley,* do I get to see Mr. Monroe or not?"

Ned glanced at her. "Jake, take your whore and go back to town."

"*No!*" Cat whirled her horse around and went galloping toward the trees.

※ ※ ※ ※

Jake recovered enough to see Ned aiming at Cat. "Shoot her and you're a dead man." He had his drawn gun trained at the foreman. "We follow her."

Ned holstered his rifle. "Whatever you say. I'll let the old man throw you both out." They headed to the path Cat had taken. When they arrived at the main house, Cat had already tied her horse to the hitching post and was knocking on the door. Jake put his gun away, and both he and Ned tied their horses. A woman answered the door and was telling Cat that Mr. Monroe wasn't at home.

Cat pulled a calling card from her pocket. "Do you have a pencil? I'd like to leave him a message."

The woman disappeared inside and returned with

one. "Here, you can use this."

Cat wrote something on the back of the card and handed it to the woman along with the pencil. "Tell him I'm at the Grand Hotel in town."

The woman glanced at the name on the card and her eyebrows rose. "I'll see he gets this."

"Thank you." Cat turned to go and came face to face with Jake. Ned stood on the steps, arms folded.

Jake grasped her arm. "Let's go. I don't think we're welcome here."

She stamped her foot. "If we aren't, it's because of you!" She pushed by him, and before he could remount, she took off on her horse again.

Ned smirked. "You sure have a handful there!" He laughed as Jake urged his horse after her.

Cat was almost to the gate when he spotted her. Her hat was bouncing on her head, the veil streaming out behind her. The girl could ride!

His horse caught up with hers, and he grabbed the reins and slowed them to a stop. "What's the matter with you? Fool woman, you're going to drive Mazie to the ground that way!"

She tried to jerk the reins out of his hand. "Let me go! Why didn't you tell me there was bad blood with my family and yours? Now I'll be lucky if I ever get to see my father!" She burst into tears.

Jake's guilt gnawed at him. "I'm sorry. I thought since I wasn't living at the Bar Seven anymore things would be different." He paused and glanced around. "There's a water trough there by that tree. The horses need a drink, and we can rest for a moment."

She let him lead the horses to the trough while she sat on a stump under the tree. He tied the reins to the post at one end of the water, and while the horses drank deeply he brought their canteens over and handed her one. "We need some, too." He sank to his haunches and was eye to eye with her. "I'll do everything in my power to get you two together, I promise."

She paused after she drank. "Why are you doing this? You barely know me, and our families don't seem to be on good terms."

"A curiosity, at first. I never heard that Monroe had a daughter. Today, I found that I genuinely like you, and I want to help." He popped the stopper onto the canteen and rose.

She glanced at him. "Jake?" Her pale green eyes were sad, and an unexpected wave of tenderness came over him. "I thought you had some sort of motive. I'm sorry I blamed you for the greeting back there." She raised her hand to him, and he helped her up.

"The horses should be ready to go." The animals had finished drinking and were pulling up wisps of grass growing by the trough. Jake and Cat mounted and turned their steeds toward town.

Back at the hotel, Cat dismounted and gave the reins to Jake. "Thank you for the use of Mazie. I hope your sister won't be upset."

"Mazie should be exercised while my sister is away, although perhaps not quite so strenuously as today. But I don't think Peggy would mind. She would probably have done the same." A twinkle in his eye, he tipped his hat. "If you need me, send word to the *Epitaph*."

As he rode to the livery stable, he wondered what he could do to let Monroe know this wasn't a trick. Maybe he should stay out of it.

After he got the horses cooled and brushed, he went to the newspaper office. Harvey glanced up from his desk. "Well? Is she the long-lost daughter?"

Jake shrugged out of his coat and tossed his hat onto a wall hook next to it. "Monroe wasn't at home, but I believe she is."

Harvey nodded. "Stay on the story. This may prove interesting when they get together."

Jake slid into the chair at his desk and took out his notepad. He tried to see the story from an uninvolved viewpoint like a good reporter should. He made more notes on what had happened that day, but he couldn't get his mind off Cat. She and her story were becoming more personal. A dangerous thing for him.

Chapter 3

As Cat quietly entered the hotel room and sat on the bed, Edna turned from putting away the clothes they hadn't sent to the laundry. "Well? Did you see him?"

Cat pulled out the pin and removed her hat, setting it beside her. "No. He wasn't at home, so I left a calling card and told the maid where I was."

Edna folded her arms. "You don't look like you believe he'll call on you."

"His foreman didn't know his boss had a daughter. And Jake's family is having a feud with them."

"I doubt having a daughter would be a topic of conversation after all this time. He hasn't even seen you since you were a babe." Edna finished up putting their garments in the hotel drawers. "We'll get the laundry back tomorrow afternoon. It's almost one thirty, and I'm sure the dining room is closed. Why don't we walk down the street to the Elite Restaurant? They have an ice cream parlor there, the laundry man said."

Cat cleaned up from the ride and put her day dress back on. After a brief walk, they arrived at a pleasant establishment with a full restaurant on one side and a coffee and dessert bar on the other. Seating themselves on the wooden stools at the counter, they each ordered an ice cream soda. Each soda arrived with a scoop of vanilla ice cream in fizzy liquid, with whipped cream and a cherry on top. A long spoon for the ice cream stuck up from one side of the tall glass, a straw on the other. In addition, a plate of wafer cookies was placed in front of them. The cool confection felt good on Cat's dust-coated throat.

Edna dipped a wafer in the ice cream and took a bite. "Mmm, at least they have some luxuries here."

Cat stirred the cream in the soda. "I hope I hear something soon. Maybe I shouldn't have left the hotel."

"I don't think there would be anything yet. You just got back."

Cat took a sip from her straw. "You're right. If it happens, though, I hope they leave a message." They finished their treats and went back to the hotel to wait.

****

A message was sent by courier to the hotel the next morning. It read:

Dear Miss Monroe,

I don't know who put you up to this, but I have no daughter. She died years ago. If this is some sort of plot cooked up by Callahan, tell that sidewinder it won't work.

Albert Monroe

Cat stood inside the door of the room to read the note, and when she had finished she let the message fall to the floor from her shaking fingers. "No! Edna!" She started to cry.

Edna hurried from the chest of drawers. "What's wrong?" She scooped up the paper. "Died?"

Cat found her handkerchief and blew her nose. "How could he think I was dead? He never wrote after he left. He never told us where he went." She paced the floor. "I have to see him, but how can I have him agree to it?"

Edna shook her head, but there was a strange look in her eyes. "I don't know, miss."

"Maybe Jake can help me somehow. He's the only friend I have here."

"How can he help if his family is in a feud with yours?"

"He might be able to help indirectly. I have to try." Cat took off her robe and gathered her clothes together. "I'm going to the newspaper office. He said to contact him there."

Edna clucked over her. "Let's have breakfast first. I'll stay here and wait for the laundry. It's supposed to be back right after lunch."

After breakfast in the dining room, Cat got directions to the *Epitaph* office. Clicking her parasol open, she hurried to Fifth Street and turned north. Words painted in black letters on the side of the building let her know she had found it, and a little brass bell on the door tinkled merrily as she went inside.

An older man with dark brown hair and graying sideburns rose from a desk and greeted her. "Morning, miss, may I help you? I'm Harvey Wilson, the editor-in-chief."

Cat nodded. "Yes. Could you tell me if Mr. Jake Spencer is in? I'm Miss Catherine Monroe."

A flash of hesitation crossed his face before he motioned to a far corner. "He's meeting with someone at this time. Can you wait a few minutes?"

She looked in the direction of the desk. Jake was in what seemed like deep conversation with a lady. Cat closed her parasol. "I'll wait."

He motioned to a caned wooden chair. "You may sit there."

Cat slid into the chair and unashamedly studied the woman with Jake. She wore a somewhat garish red-and-white-striped dress and too much jewelry for this time of the morning. Her hat carried a tall arched red ostrich feather. Mr. Wilson spoke to Jake, pointing in Cat's direction, and Cat immediately studied a fly on the ceiling. When she glanced back as the woman rose to leave, her glance took in not only the side of her painted face but a glimpse of the striped dress front. The neckline was so low the rise of her bosoms blossomed over the material like puddings. Cat wanted to blast her to kingdom come. Jealousy? Why was she jealous?

Jake came over. "Cat! What may I do for you?"

Unexpected warmth came over her, and her chest tightened. "Something came up, and I wanted to talk to you."

He led her to his desk. "Please sit down."

Cat tried to ignore the smell of strong perfume from its former occupant. She took out the courier letter from her reticule and showed it to him. "This came to the hotel this morning."

A puzzled expression set his features. "You're supposed to be dead?"

"I don't know where he got that. I don't believe he ever wrote to us after he left, so we had nowhere to send any news to him, let alone false information."

"What do you want me to do?"

"I was hoping you could come up with an idea on how I could meet him."

Jake paused. "I have been thinking about your problem. You saw the woman I was talking to?"

Cat's jaw tightened. "Yes, I did."

"I knew she has been seeing Daniel Monroe on a regular basis. She works at the Bird Cage Theater, and he usually comes to the Friday night performances."

Cat perked up. "That's tonight! Where is this place? I want to go."

Jake's mouth set in a tight line. "There's something you must know. The Bird Cage is *not* a respectable theater. I wasn't going to tell you I was going to go tonight myself to see if I could talk him into meeting you."

Her eyes widened. "A den of iniquity?"

"That's putting it mildly."

Her curiosity made her a bit bold. "Have—have you been there before?"

He grinned. "And what if I have?" Her cheeks burned. "The best place to sort through the gossip is at the source. If you're asking if I ever participated in the business, the answer is no. Too many diseases hang around there. Dara is one of my informants to nose out the news, that's all."

"What are you going to tell Daniel?"

"That you want to see him. I'll send a message to the hotel tomorrow morning if I'm successful and find a place for the two of you to meet."

Cat rose and held out her hand. "Thank you, Jake. You've been most kind."

He clasped her hand, and an electric current went up her arm. "Pleased to be of service, Cat."

She hurried out, suddenly feeling warmer than she had before. What was wrong? She'd visited with young men in the past, and none of them had ever affected her this way. She found herself at ease with Jake, yet he caused her body to do the strangest things.

Opening her parasol, Cat turned back to the hotel.

****

Jake shrugged on his suit coat and made sure he had enough coin to go to the theater. A couple of beers wouldn't fuzz his brain but would look real enough to let others open up to him.

The noise hit him before he crossed the street to enter the establishment. No one in there talked below a roar. The smell of cheap cigars and stale booze permeated the air as he edged his way to the bar in the gambling den of the theater. Since most men got their pay on Fridays, the urge to get more money lured them here. Miners and cowboys vied to see who could lose more at the faro tables. Often a fight over something would break out.

He stood at the large mahogany bar, its mirrors reflecting the chaos, and ordered a beer. The cold glass was set in front of him. As he took a mouthful of the bitter draft, he felt someone step up beside him.

"Jake?"

He turned to a young man with ground-in dirt on his exposed skin. "Daniel. Been a long time."

"Yeah." Daniel wiped his nose with his sleeve. "Dara said you wanted to see me."

Jake motioned toward a vacant table. "Bring your drink over there. Let's talk." He settled into a wooden chair and leaned toward Daniel so he could be heard over the din. "Two days ago, a lady named Catherine Monroe arrived in town claiming that Albert is her father."

"Well, she's a liar. I don't have a sister."

"Your father said in a letter to her that his daughter was dead."

26

Daniel nodded. "That's what I always heard."

"Can I at least get you to meet with the young lady and listen to her? She does resemble you," Jake remarked, taking in the sable brown hair and pale green eyes.

Daniel shrugged. "No skin off my nose. When?"

"How about dinner at the Elite tomorrow night? Eight o'clock? My treat."

"Yeah, all right." Daniel pushed back and stood up. "Going into the theater. Are you?"

"No, not tonight. I'll see you at the restaurant tomorrow." Jake walked with him to the theater entrance, where loud rinky-dink music came from a trio of piano, banjo, and fiddle players. As Daniel went through the door, Jake caught sight of the cages with the business girls in various stages of undress, gyrating to the music. A den of iniquity, indeed.

As Jake was leaving, two combatants tumbled from the gambling den and went on punching each other outside. He stepped back and waited. Scuffling noises told him they continued their dispute. Several horses stomped and whinnied, and then he heard a shot. A number of patrons were gathered, watching the spectacle. Jake slipped out the side door and went up to where a crowd stood gawking as a sheriff's deputy ran across the street. Just another Friday night in Tombstone.

Jake supposed he should get the particulars for the newspaper. He removed his notebook and got the names and the what-for, then continued on his way.

He sat on the outside bench by the Oriental Saloon and rolled himself a cigarette. Watching the smoke curl up into the dark sky, he thought about Cat. He'd only known her a couple of days, but he felt like he'd known her a lifetime. The little minx didn't realize how much she'd aroused him by asking bold questions at the office. The women at the Bird Cage didn't hold any fascination for him this evening. He usually would stop in for a few minutes to watch them. Not that he ever took part in the pleasures. He'd had a couple of experiences with girls, growing up, but those hadn't lasted.

His cigarette finished, Jake dropped the butt on the walk and rubbed it out with the toe of his shoe. Standing, he turned toward his apartment and anticipated seeing Cat tomorrow.

Chapter 4

At their table in the hotel dining room, Cat waved a piece of paper at Edna. "Jake saw my brother Daniel last night, who agreed to have dinner with us this evening! Jake will escort us to the Elite Restaurant at a quarter to eight, and we will meet Daniel there."

Edna's mouth formed a tight line. "Mr. Spencer is inserting himself too much in our affairs."

"Edna! He's just trying to help me."

"That may be so, but he's probably going to expect something in return. You may regret it."

Cat set the napkin on her lap as their breakfast order arrived. "And you worry too much. Stop being so suspicious of everyone."

Once back in their room, Cat shook out her good blue dinner dress. "This is the one with the loose hem. Where's the sewing kit? I'll have to fix it."

Edna rummaged in her trunk and pulled out a leather case. "Here it is. I could do that for you."

Cat shook her head. "This will keep me busy for a while. You know how I hate to sit around."

Edna gave her a quick glance. "I'm the one who's had to wait around this hotel."

Cat settled into a chair by the window. "I am sorry about that. Why don't you make a list of what we need and go to some of the shops around here?" She gathered some money out of her trunk and gave it to Edna.

"Good idea." Edna took an inventory and, with Cat's approval of the list, left on her errand.

Cat set to work but found herself looking out the window over Allen Street, watching carriages and horses come and go. The sun warmed her as she sewed, and as the morning grew hotter, she opened the windows a bit.

Her mind kept wandering to Jake. Why was he so interested in helping her? Could it be, like Edna said, he was expecting something in return? He was handsome. It's a wonder some girl hadn't snatched him up by now. Was it unseemly to wonder what it would be like to kiss him? She closed her eyes and had a tingling low in her belly. Then she forced herself down to earth. No good taking herself on these flights of fancy.

She finished her sewing and hung the dress to pull out the wrinkles, since she didn't have an iron. Picking up a *Godey's Ladies Book* purchased at the Union News Depot, she settled in to read for a while.

****

Jake went through his wardrobe to find his dinner jacket and shook it out. It had been a while since he'd had an outing with a young lady, even though it wasn't officially courting. He hung the jacket up and took a clothes brush to it.

A knock—well, a banging—came on his door, as did a shout of "Jake!" He opened it, and his father stood there looking mad enough to bite a rattler. "What in the land of Beelzebub are you up to? Ned Hadley came roaring to the ranch and told me you brought over a little floozy who claimed she was Monroe's daughter. He said if either of you show your face at Sugar Springs again, he'll blow your fool head off."

"Whoa, Pa, simmer down! First off, Miss Monroe is no floozy, and she has enough evidence to her story that I believe her."

"Even if she does, why are you messing around with the Monroes?" He pointed an accusing finger at Jake. "Remember, they're the ones stealing our water."

Jake sighed. "No one knows that for sure."

"There's one thing I know for sure: my boy's gone over to the enemy. First you hightail it into town to become a *newsman*, and then you take up with a Monroe. How much worse can it get?"

"Pa, this has nothing whatsoever to do with you or Callahan."

His father clamped his hat on his head and turned to go. "We'll see. We'll just see." He slammed the door behind him.

Jake poured a glass of whiskey from a flask on his side table. *Things are starting to boil again after an uneasy truce. Cat's not aware of the trouble she's stirred up, coming here.* He hoped he could keep a cap on the charge before it blew them all sky high.

He turned up at the hotel dressed to the gills, and when he knocked on the door of Cat's room, she opened it and stood there looking gorgeous. Warmth flooded his body and stiffened his groin. He took a deep breath. "Are you two ladies ready?"

Cat and Edna acknowledged him and tied their shoulder capes, he offered an arm to each, and they walked to the restaurant. He noticed a trembling on Cat's part. *Nerves, probably.* This would be her chance to lay her case to a family member. Edna was as stoic as ever.

Daniel wasn't at the restaurant yet. Jake had just

settled the ladies at a table, when he noticed Daniel coming in. He excused himself to greet his friend, who had managed to scrub up pretty well. Daniel leaned toward Jake. "Which one is she?"

"The one in blue."

"A real looker, ain't she?" He removed his hat and smoothed back his hair. Jake preceded him to the table.

****

Out of the corner of her eye, Cat watched Jake lead a young man to them. She took a deep breath to quiet her nerves, then looked up and smiled.

Jake motioned to the man. "Mr. Daniel Monroe, may I present Miss Catherine Monroe and Miss Edna Harper."

Cat extended her hand. "Pleased to meet you. You may call me Cat." She wanted to cry and throw her arms around him, but she managed to stay reserved.

Daniel shook it. "A pleasure, Cat."

A waiter came over. "Are you ready to order?"

Jake glanced at Daniel. "Should I order for all of us?"

Daniel nodded. "Anything's all right with me."

Jake read the menu. "We'll start with oysters and salad. Then stuffed quail with rolls and vegetables. Finish that up with a plate of ice cream." He looked at the others. "White wine?"

Cat spoke up. "Edna doesn't drink alcohol."

Edna removed her gloves. "I'll have tea and lemon."

Jake turned to the waiter. "Tea and lemon for Miss Harper, and the rest will have white wine."

The waiter gave a quick bow. "Yes, sir."

Daniel studied Cat. "Miss Monroe—"

"Call me Cat," she interjected.

"All right. Cat, what makes you believe you're my sister?"

"I was born in Alexandria, Virginia, in 1864, to Lettie Monroe. My father, Albert, was a major in Robert E. Lee's army, Longstreet's Division. My mother died a few months after I was born. I and my two brothers, John and Daniel, went to live with my mother's sister, Camille, and her husband, Leland. From what I've been told, my father, when he mustered out of the army after the war, didn't want to live under the Federals, so he took his sons and moved west. John was five years old and Daniel two. Aunt Camille didn't think the west was a good place to raise a girl, so she kept me. Now will you tell me about your family?"

Daniel registered shock. "You seem to know it already." Suspicion crept into his eyes. "How do I know you didn't find this out from somebody? Do you have any proof?"

"I have a document of birth notarized from the Clerk of Records at the Alexandria courthouse, and a tintype of my mother." She produced a small picture and gave it to him.

He studied it as their oysters and drinks arrived. "That looks like the one Pa has, for sure."

Cat was encouraged that he was almost convinced. "Daniel, do you know who told your pa I was dead?"

He shook his head. "That's what I was always told." He paused for a moment. "Can you tell me anything that only family would know? For instance, what's my middle name? I never use it, so only family would know that."

Cat hesitated. She had seen tintypes of her brothers

from those early years, and all of their birth dates, recorded by Aunt Camille in the family Bible. Reviewing the memory in her mind, it came to her. "Ezra! Your middle name is Ezra."

The oyster shell he held clattered to his plate. Daniel rose and went to her side, drawing her into a bear hug. "You have to be Catherine, my baby sister!"

Cat, overwhelmed, sobbed on his shoulder. "You believe me!" After a minute, she pulled back. "Do you think you can convince our father?"

Daniel paused. "They always have Sunday supper in the big house after they return from church. We'll go there tomorrow."

"What church do they attend?"

"St. Paul's, here in town."

"I'd like to go."

"I'll tell you what. I'll rent a rig tomorrow morning, and we can go to church, then to the ranch. Edna can come along, too."

Cat threw her arms back around his neck. "Thank you, oh, thank you!"

He stepped back and grasped her shoulders. "I have to tell you, though—I'm not in good graces with the family."

Cat's stomach tightened. "What do you mean?"

He gazed at the toe of his shoe. "You've heard of the prodigal son? Well, you're looking at the Monroe version." He sighed. "I never liked ranch work and kept fighting with Pa and John. I up and walked out one day, demanding from Pa my share of the holdings. I got a job working in the silver mines. I'm not what you call a real upstanding citizen."

Cat's dream was starting to crumble. "You mean

Father might not believe you, either?"

He shook his head. "Bring that picture and your document of birth. If you can answer all the questions, maybe he will."

Their stuffed quail was served, but Cat did little more than pick at it. To come all this way, searching for her family, and they didn't believe her. Who had told her father she was dead? The scenario she imagined was an overjoyed father welcoming his long-lost daughter into the bosom of his family, not this.

She somehow got through dinner and left with the promise to be ready when Daniel came to take them to church. Jake escorted the ladies back to the hotel.

In the lobby, he turned to Cat. "May I speak with you?"

Edna glanced up. "I'll go up to our room. Thank you, and goodnight, Mr. Spencer."

"You're welcome. Goodnight, Miss Harper."

When she left, Cat said, "What is it?"

He reached for her hand and clasped it. "Cat, I'm sorry. I didn't know things were that way between Daniel and his family. I wanted to help."

She smiled. "I know, and I am grateful to you. You've been very kind." They were standing almost nose to nose, and suddenly her cheeks heated. She let go of his hand. "Thank you for dinner. I have to go now." She headed toward the stairs.

"Cat?"

"Goodnight, Jake." Her body was doing those strange things again. If she stayed with him any longer, she wouldn't be able to say goodbye, for fear of what he made her feel.

Chapter 5

Cat picked at the lace on her glove as she and Edna waited in the lobby for Daniel to arrive. A surrey stopped at the entrance, and Daniel came in to greet them. He was wearing the same suit he'd worn last night.

"Are you ready to go?" he asked.

Cat laid a hand on his arm. "Yes, but I don't think we should try to go to the ranch without being invited. I want to talk to them after church."

"Anything you say." He helped Cat and Edna into the surrey and the horses started up at his command. A few streets over, they arrived at St. Paul's, the town's Episcopal church. It was a handsome building of adobe and brick.

Daniel escorted both the ladies through the tall wooden doors and into the whitewashed interior, where a pump organ was playing "Onward, Christian Soldiers." Cat thought this was appropriate because she felt like a soldier going to battle. Once they had found an open pew in the back and sat down, Cat took her Book of Common Prayer out of her reticule and clutched it tightly. The sun through the stained glass windows made colorful patterns on the opposite wall.

Daniel leaned toward Cat. "There they are, by the window on the other side."

She glanced toward the sunny side of the room and

saw a tall man with graying hair seating himself on the aisle. Next to him was a young couple with a little boy and girl. "Is that John's family?"

He nodded. "John's wife is Polly. The children are Sam and Aggie."

A warm glow came over Cat. "I'm an aunt." She longed to hold the children. A real family!

The morning prayers and the sermon went by too slowly. Finally came the closing hymn, and the priest, readers, and servers filed out of the church. Being in the back pew, Daniel and Cat were out first. The priest's hand grasped hers. "You're new here. You are?"

"Catherine. I arrived in town this week."

He clapped Daniel on the shoulder. "I haven't seen you here for a while. Are you escorting the young lady?"

Daniel hesitated. "Her and her companion, Edna."

The priest greeted Edna. "Welcome to you, too. Do you plan to stay long?"

Edna glanced at Cat. "Perhaps."

The three stood to the side, waiting for the Monroes to come out. Albert Monroe stalked toward them with a scowl. "What do you mean, bringing your women to church? Have you no shame?"

Anger clouded Daniel's features. "As usual, you don't know what you're talking about, Pa. She claims to be your daughter, Catherine Monroe, and I believe her."

Albert whirled on her. "You're the one who came by last week with the Spencer boy?"

Cat opened and closed her mouth, then said, "Yes."

"Lady, I don't know what you're trying to pull, but it won't work. I sent you the letter to the hotel about my

37

daughter."

"But you're wrong! I have proof."

She handed him the tintype. "This is my mother, Lettie Monroe." A folded paper came out of her reticule next. "Here's my record of birth."

He thrust them back at her. "Anyone could have gotten these."

Daniel cut in. "Pa, she knew my middle name!"

Albert turned on him. "She could have gotten that where she got the picture and the record."

She tearfully retrieved the picture that had slipped to the ground. "I did! From my Uncle Leland and Aunt Camille. They raised me."

"Then why did I get a letter from Camille telling me my daughter had died?"

Horror filled her soul. "I don't know."

He turned on his heel and strode to the carriage where his family was waiting for him. Cat tried to follow, but he was out of the lot before she could catch up. Tears blinded her as she ran toward the hotel. She heard a shout and ran into a solid body that grasped her shoulders. "Cat!"

Jake had her. "Let go of me! Why are you always where I am? Are you following me?" She wriggled to free herself.

"Catherine, did it occur to you that I might go to St. Paul's too?" He drew her to him.

She flailed with her arms and legs but finally quieted and sobbed on his shoulder. "Why can't he believe me?" Between sobs, she told him about the letter from her aunt. His comforting arms felt so good around her.

By then, Daniel and Edna had gotten into the

surrey and pulled up beside them, where Daniel handed the reins to Edna and hopped out. "I'm sorry Pa acted like that. I guess I was the wrong one to try and convince him."

Jake stepped back and cradled her chin in his hand. "Is there anyone back in Virginia who could provide proof?"

Cat went over in her mind who could help her. "I could write to Ben. He got the house when my uncle and aunt passed away. He was two years older than John and should remember when we came to live with them."

Jake nodded. "Good. Only have him write directly to Albert Monroe. That way he can't accuse you of faking it."

"Thank you, I will." She gave him a quick hug, and he helped her into the surrey. They held hands for a moment longer before he gave her fingers a squeeze and let go.

He tipped his hat. "You're welcome."

Daniel climbed in and took the reins from Edna, slapped the straps on the horses' backs, and headed to the hotel. After dropping them off, Daniel turned to Cat. "I hope this works. I know I'm happy you showed up. I like having a sister."

She gave his cheek a peck. "Thank you for that. I'm happy to have found you." With their goodbyes, Cat and Edna went upstairs to their room, where Cat composed a letter to Ben.

Dear Ben,

I hope this finds everyone in your family well. I have found my father after a long search, but he does not believe me. He told me your mother wrote to him that I was dead. I have a request—Could you write to him? Being two years older than my brother John, you must remember when we came to live with your family. Let him know I am the same girl as the one who came with her brothers. Please send the letter directly to him, Albert Monroe, in care of Sugar Springs Ranch, NE Tombstone, Arizona Territory. I will be most grateful to you.

Your cousin,
Cat

She sealed her letter in a carefully addressed envelope and purchased a stamp from the man at the front desk. "Could you see that this goes out first thing tomorrow?"

He placed it in a mail sack. "Yes, ma'am."

She and Edna slipped into the dining room for a late breakfast.

****

Monday morning, Jake hung up his coat and hat and slid into his chair behind his desk. He took out his file on the Monroe story and began to record notes. Someone leaned against the top of his compartment, and Jake looked up.

Harvey picked up one of the sheets. "So what's new on that Monroe girl? I heard there was a commotion outside St. Paul's that you were involved with yesterday."

"She confronted Albert with her evidence, and he didn't believe her."

"Are you going to write up the story yet?"

"Not now. The story isn't complete. Anyway, I don't want to give wind to Albert on what she is going to try next."

Harvey's face grew grave. "I think you're getting too involved with that Monroe girl. I may have to take you off it."

"Why? Because I've tried to help her?" Jake wanted to do everything to protect Cat. His fist beat a rhythm on the arm of his chair.

"Many people saw you holding the girl after the confrontation, apparently comforting her. Some found it quite scandalous."

"Damn it! She was upset and ran into me. What was I supposed to do? Throw her to the ground?"

"All right, Jake, I'm leaving you on for now. You have to remember, a good newsman reports the news, not makes it." He strode back to his desk while Jake seethed.

Jake wrote up the news tidbits he had jotted down from around town and gave the copy to the typesetters. After he delivered that, he got ready to leave on his news rounds.

Harvey cornered him before Jake got out the door. "Maybe I was too hasty with my advice. Having someone on the inside of the story might be a good thing." He handed Jake two tickets. "Here's admission to the Last Rose of Summer Ball at Schieffelin Hall in two weeks. I want a report on the evening."

Jake gave him a long look. "Harvey, this is two tickets. I assume I can invite anyone I like?"

Harvey paused. "That's right."

"You flop around worse than a fish out of water. You just about tore my head off for helping *that Monroe girl.*"

"Callahan and the Monroes usually attend the balls. Your story may have some added information before the night is out."

"In other words, none of the other papers have an inkling about this. My, Harvey, you *are* a mercenary." Jake jammed his hat on and pushed his way out. Part of him was angry, but there was an equal or more part that looked forward to escorting Miss Monroe to the ball. He realized he wanted any excuse to be able to be with her. Winding his way to Allen Street, he stepped into the entrance of the Grand Hotel. He greeted the desk clerk. "Good morning, Ed. Anything new today?"

Ed adjusted his glasses as he checked the register. "No. The stage hasn't come in yet."

"Could you send a message to Miss Monroe in Room Ten and ask if she'll have the midday meal with me here in the dining room?"

Ed rang the bell on the desk and a bellboy appeared. "Yes, sir?"

Jake wrote the message on a calling card, and Ed put it a tray. "Take this up to Miss Monroe in Room Ten."

The bellboy picked up the small delivery plate from the desk and was back in a moment with the reply that she would be down in fifteen minutes. Jake sat on one of the red velvet lobby chairs to wait.

When Cat came downstairs, she wore a plain gray day dress with a high starched collar. With her hair pinned loosely on the sides but left to cascade down her back in rich brown curls, she seemed much younger. She smiled when she saw him, and the heat scorched his innards. "I'd love to dine with you."

He offered his arm, and they strolled into the dining room, which was starting to serve the midday meal. He ordered tea, sandwiches, and fruit compote for both of them. "Did you get your letter posted this morning?"

She nodded. "First thing. I hope this works. My father seems like a very suspicious man."

"He's had a lot of problems since he bought the Sugar Springs ranch ten years ago. I was still living at the Bar Seven at the time. Old Man Callahan kept saying that the spring didn't flow as well as it did before, and he accused Monroe of diverting the water, but that was never proved."

"The feud seems to be still going on." She gazed at him. "Knowing I was a Monroe, why did you decide to try to help me?"

"Since I moved to town, I don't consider myself part of that mess anymore." He gazed at her. "And I find you a most fascinating woman."

Her blush was beautiful. "Jake, please, not in public." Their meal was delivered, and Jake almost forgot why he had come to see her.

"Cat, would you do me the honor of accompanying me to the Last Rose of Summer Ball at the Schieffelin Hall the first Saturday in September?"

She stopped in mid bite. "A formal affair? I don't know—"

"Usually the Monroes show up for the balls. They might receive a letter from your cousin by then." Jake held his breath.

She tapped her compote bowl with her spoon for a moment. "The gown I carry with me is a couple of seasons old, and I don't know if there's enough time for me to commission a new one."

"I could see if my sister—"

"No, I can't keep borrowing her things just because

43

she's away. Can I give you an answer tomorrow?"

Jake tightened his mouth. He hadn't thought this would be difficult. Women! He sighed. "We'll meet here same time tomorrow. Will that give you enough time to decide?"

She gave him a dazzling smile that cut into his exasperation. "Oh, yes. I'd love to have another meal with you."

Jake was looking forward to it as well.

****

After thanking Jake for the midday repast, Cat hurried up to her room. "Edna, could you find my ball gown?"

Edna looked up from her mending. "Whatever for?"

Cat picked up her magazines and searched for the fashion plates. "Jake invited me to a ball in two weeks, and I've got to find something suitable to wear."

Rummaging through Cat's trunk, Edna emerged with a pale yellow gown wrapped in tissue paper. Cat held it up by the shoulders and studied it critically. Edna glanced at one of the fashion plates and back at the dress. "The bodice is suitable, but it has very little bustle."

Cat nodded. "And the skirt is straighter than the fashion now, with too much bric-a-brac on it. You know, we could take that all off and get more material to drape a bustle."

Edna pointed at one of the gowns. "We could add some material on either side of the skirt to make it fuller, too."

"Yes, yes! And I'm sure we can have it done in two weeks!" She held the dress to her shoulders and gazed in the mirror; then she whirled around the room. "I'll accept Jake's invitation tomorrow, and then I will go shopping for material."

She found her sewing scissors and sat down to strip the lace, bows, and flowers off the skirt. Dancing with Jake entered her dreams that night.

Chapter 6

The small brass bell on the door tinkled merrily as Cat came into the California Variety Store. The fragrance of spices in wooden bins caught her nose, along with that of several bushels of early apples, which must have been shipped from the mountains. She clutched her large basket, looking around the shop, and spotted the shelves with a colorful array of material bolts. A thin-faced man poked around at a notions counter, then glanced at Cat. "May I help you, miss?"

She set her basket on the counter. "Yes. I'd like to buy some taffeta fabric." She dug into the basket and pulled out a swatch she had cut off the dress when she altered it. "I'd like material in a similar pale yellow, and a pale green, as well."

He took the swatch and ran his finger down the bolts, searching for the right ones. He took two off the shelves and set them in front of her. "These are the finest taffetas, straight from New York." He unrolled a little to let her feel it.

She studied the yellow closely, holding the swatch next to it. "Yes, this should work." She held the green with the swatch. "Do you have a pale lime green? The olive just won't do."

He removed the bolt of olive green fabric and found a green more to her liking. "How many yards do you desire?"

Cat took out a piece of paper. "I want four of the yellow and seven of the green." While he measured the material on the yardstick affixed to the counter, she checked through the notions. "And I'd like twelve yards of the green gorse ribbon, too."

After the clerk finished measuring her order, he pulled a pencil from behind his ear and wrote her sales slip. "Will that be all?" At her nod, he continued, "Let's see. Taffeta is five cents a yard, and the ribbon is two." He worked the figures. "That will be seventy-nine cents."

She paid the bill and deposited the brown paper packages in her basket. The bell repeated its performance as she went out into the sunshine. Turning toward the hotel, she opened her parasol against the midday sun. A place called the Wine Rooms loomed ahead and, as Cat approached it, the doors flew open and two combatants knocked the basket out of her hands as they continued their brawling. Her packages landed in the dusty street and were stepped on by the angry men.

Cat lowered her parasol and cracked one of the oafs on the back of the neck. "Get off my purchases!"

He grabbed the parasol and jerked her toward him. "Hey, missy, what do you think you're doing?" His breath smelled like beer and onions as his dirty fingers clasped her shoulder.

"Unhand me, you brute!" She was shaken, and out of the corner of her eye, she saw a figure fly out of the barroom. Daniel pulled the man away.

"Leave the lady alone!" Daniel growled. He rested his hand on his holstered gun.

The man hesitated, most of the fight drained out of

him. "All right. I'm backing up."

"I suggest you pick up her packages and apologize."

The man glared at them both. Picking up the items, he thrust them into her hands. "Sorry, ma'am." He looked around, but the man he'd been fighting with had disappeared, so he turned on his heel and made his way down the street while the spectators returned to what they had been doing.

Straightening her hat, Cat inspected the material. "The packages seem intact. How opportune that you happened to be here."

Daniel checked her up and down. "Are you hurt?" At the shake of her head, he continued, "I usually have lunch here. They have a spread that you can eat at the price of a beer."

Cat opened her parasol. "Thank you for your help."

"Just be careful. This isn't Alexandria. Most carry guns here." He went back into the barroom, and Cat headed for the hotel.

Edna clucked at her. "What happened to you? You're covered with dust."

"I had an unfortunate encounter with a couple of roughnecks who spilled out of a bar on my way back. Luckily, Daniel happened to be there and chased them off." She opened one of the packages and shook out the material. It didn't look the worse for wear.

"I hope those ruffians don't hold a grudge."

Cat waved her off. "I don't think I was anything but an interruption in their fight." She paged through her fashion plates until she found the style of gown she wanted. "Do you think you could do the drape like this?"

Edna peered at the plate. "I'm sure I can. Slip the gown on, and I'll start pinning."

As Cat removed her dress, there was a gnaw in the back of her mind about the man she'd hit, but she thrust that to a deep corner and concentrated on the task at hand.

****

Jake spent several days seeing the delightful Miss Monroe at midday at the hotel. He looked forward to their conversations. The lady was well educated, and her tastes were similar to his. Since his move to town he'd learned much about theater and music, mainly on different assignments to social events. He checked his watch. Still a half hour to noon.

Harvey appeared at his desk. "Jake, it seems your friend Daniel Monroe is in a heap of trouble with Whiskey Jones, a hand over at the Bar Seven."

"Why?"

"A few days ago, what he called an upstart female hit him on the back of the head when he ran into her. Daniel came out of the Wine Rooms and threatened him with a gun. Now he swears he's going to shoot Daniel next time he sees him."

A sinking feeling enclosed Jake. "Any idea who the female was?"

"Knowing how reluctant Daniel is to get into trouble when he's sober, I'd say it was either Dara or that Monroe girl."

Jake felt lightheaded. "I remember Whiskey never did take well to being threatened. I'd better alert Daniel."

"Has Miss Monroe heard anything from Albert?"

"I don't think there's been time enough to get a

49

reply back from the letter she sent to her cousin. I'm hoping there will be something before the ball."

Harvey pounded on the desk with his fingers. "I expect some kind of story on this after the ball. With the way things are going, one of the other newspapers is going to get wind of it. Understood?"

Jake slumped a little. "Yes, sir."

Jake was more than a little annoyed at Cat when he met her for their usual midday meal. They sat at a table in the dining room, and Jake ordered poached eggs on toast, with ham and fruit sauce, for both of them.

Cat removed her gloves and gazed at him, her green eyes full of questions. "Something is bothering you today. What is it?"

Jake leveled a stern stare at her. "Why didn't you tell me about the fight a few days ago?"

"Fight?" She looked blankly at him; then the dawn came. "Oh, you mean those two ruffians who ran into me? How did you know about that?"

"My editor told me. I guessed it was you." He went on to let her know about the threat against Daniel. "This isn't Virginia. You have to be careful who you rile up around here."

She took all that in. "So Daniel is truly in trouble because of me?"

"Well, Whiskey doesn't come to town that often, but he doesn't forget, either."

"Would it help if I apologize to Mr. Jones?"

Jake shook his head. "I don't think so. His dander is up against Daniel."

Her face darkened as their order came. "Oh, dear, I didn't mean to get him into this."

"Daniel chose to defend you. It's not your fault."

Cat picked at her food. "If you see him, please tell him to be careful."

"He can take care of himself. Don't worry, but try to stay out of trouble yourself."

After they parted, Jake wasn't terribly reassured. As he went on his rounds collecting news tidbits, the worry over Cat and her brother gnawed at him. He turned in at the Bird Cage Theater and found Dara in the bar. She was swirling a drink in a glass when he slid into an empty seat next to her.

She glanced at him. "Howdy, handsome. Trolling for an open port?"

He gave her a half-smile. "Still trying to get me as a customer, huh?"

"Most of what we get here aren't the best-looking hombres. A gal can dream." She took a drink from her glass. "What can I do for you?"

"I heard Whiskey Jones isn't too pleased with Daniel Monroe. Could you tell Daniel to stay out of his way?"

"Yeah, I heard he played Sir Galahad for his sister. She sure has been stirring things up since she came to town."

Jake's hand slammed on the table. "She was merely trying to find her family. It's not her fault they're a bunch of jackasses."

"Sounds like you want a warm little Southern—"

"Dara!"

She gave him a smirk, then took another drink. "I'll give Daniel your message."

Jake jammed on his hat and left without another word. He couldn't tell Dara how right she was.

****

Two days before the ball, Cat and Edna put the finishing touches on the altered ball gown, taking advantage of the morning sun. A knock on the door interrupted their work. Cat opened it to a messenger boy with a card on a tray.

"Miss Monroe? A gentleman is in the lobby to see you."

She took the calling card, and saw the name Albert Monroe emblazoned on it. Her chest tightened. "Tell Mr. Monroe I'll be down in only a few moments." She put one of her cards on the tray. When the boy was gone, with one of her nickels, she turned to Edna. "He must have heard from Ben."

Edna glanced up from her sewing. "Do you want me to come with you?"

Cat shook her head. "No, I can handle it." She took off the scarf she'd used to tie back her long hair. Taking three combs, she affixed her curls back from her face, leaving a cascade hanging down her back.

As she approached the stairs to the lobby, her stomach tightened. Her hand closed around the banister, and she hesitated. She wasn't sure what he was going to say. Putting her hand on her aching midsection, she stood watching her father, seated on a chair within view of the stairs.

Albert looked up, and many emotions played on his face. Surprise and sorrow were major among them. He rose as she gathered herself and started down with a great lump lodged in her throat and tears burning her eyes.

He met Cat at the bottom and held her by the shoulders. "I should have known. You are so much like your mother." They embraced, and Cat let loose the tide she'd been holding back.

Neither could speak for a few moments as Cat sobbed on his rough jacket and Albert rocked her. She pulled back and shook out her handkerchief. "You believe me now?"

He dried his face with his own. "I received a letter from Ben in Virginia. I knew you probably set that up, and I came to tell you so, but then I really saw you like I hadn't before."

They went to an empty corner of the lobby and sat on one of the couches. Cat smiled. "I'm so happy you believe me now."

Albert glanced down. "I was sure you were out to get some inheritance, masquerading as my daughter."

"I'm not interested in your money. I wanted to find you after Aunt and Uncle died. Ben inherited the house, and I felt I wasn't welcome to stay there anymore. I was left enough money to live on, so I went searching for you."

"By yourself?"

"No. My maid came with me as a traveling companion." She was silent for a moment. "What made you think I was dead?"

"After I purchased Sugar Springs, ten years ago, I wrote your Aunt Camille to send for you. I thought this could be a stable home, but that's the answer I received."

Stunned, Cat stared at him. "Why would Auntie do something like that?"

He frowned, then shook his head. "I don't know. Maybe to keep you from moving west."

Conflicting emotions roiled in her head. She had been hurt, sure her father had forgotten about her. Now the hurt was a new one, finding out her aunt didn't tell her about her father's letter. "I'm sorry I felt so angry that you never wrote. I was blaming you."

"I want to make it up to you. I want you and your maid to come live at the ranch until you find a suitor."

Cat hesitated. "Can I think about this? I could give you an answer next week. I do thank you for your kind offer, but I've enjoyed taking care of myself these past few months."

"An unmarried woman shouldn't be on her own. People around here will think the worst."

"I've been here for almost a month. It seems the die is already cast."

"Besides," came a voice from behind them, "how else can I take my midday meal with her?"

"Jake Spencer," Albert said through clenched teeth. "I was told you were with her when she rode to the ranch."

Cat put a hand on Albert's arm. "Jake has been a friend to me from the first."

He ignored her. "Did old man Callahan or your father put you up to this?"

Jake shook his head. "No, sir. I haven't lived at the Bar Seven for over a year. In fact, I got stampeded by my father for seeing her."

"You've been seeing her?"

"Yes. We're going to the ball this coming Saturday."

"Not if I have anything to say about it!"

A prick of anger stabbed at her. "You don't, Father. I've already accepted his offer."

Albert rose and put on his hat. "This was the way you were raised? To defy your parents?"

"I think I know about substance of character. There is nothing wrong with Jake."

"Excuse me!" Albert stalked out of the hotel.

Frustrated tears rolled down her cheek. She stood and stomped her foot. "He acknowledged he was my father, and we were getting along so well until you came in!"

Jake held both her hands and squeezed gently. "Cat, you defended me. And to a father you've been searching so long for. You must feel something for me."

Confusion ripped her apart. What Jake said was all too true. What was the matter with her? "Jake, I—I couldn't let a father I never knew tell me who I can and can't see." She squeezed his hands back. "You have been so kind to me since I've been here, I couldn't let him do that."

He released her and ran his fingers over a strand of her hair. "I love your hair down. You have beautiful silky curls."

Her cheeks burned. "I should put it up before we go to the dining room."

"No, leave it down today. I'm sure you won't cause a scandal if you don't pin it up." He offered her his arm. "Shall we?"

As Cat took it, those strange but very pleasant vibrations surged through her body. He glanced at her and grinned. Her spine liquefied. She wanted to be a part of him.

Chapter 7

Jake cursed as he retied the formal tie again. He'd lost count of how many times he'd redone it already, wanting everything to be perfect for Cat tonight. He stared at the reflection in the mirror of his washstand. "Admit it. You've fallen so far for that Monroe girl you may never be found again."

The thought crossed his mind that he should give the reporting notes to someone else to write about the Monroes, but he didn't know if Harvey would agree to it. Jake had been warned many times not to get close to his subjects. Now he was.

He hurried down the outside steps to the livery across the street. "Hey, Jim, got the rig set up for me?"

The tall blond man motioned toward the back room. "I have it back there. Seems everybody is renting rigs for the ball tonight."

"Thanks. Just name a favor when you need it." He gave Jim five dollars. "Keep the change."

Jim tipped his sweat-stained hat. "Welcome. Good evening to you."

Stepping into the back room, Jake walked around the rig as Jim opened the side doors of the building. Jake scratched the nose of the black horse harnessed up. "Shadow, good to see you, boy." The horse nickered as Jake produced a sugar cube from his coat pocket. After giving the horse a treat, he hopped onto the driver's seat, slapped the reins, and let Shadow take him down the drive to the street. It took hardly any time to arrive at the hotel. Tying the rig to the hitching post, he went in for Cat.

He slipped his calling card onto one of the messenger's trays, and the boy took it up while Jake leaned on one of the pillars to wait. The boy came back with one of her cards and told him she'd be right down.

A vision greeted his eyes at the top of the stairs— Cat in a white lace waist-length cape over a yellow-and-green gown. A white-gloved hand rested lightly on the banister with a white reticule and fan hanging from her wrist. Her hair was pinned up into a green ribbon, with frizzy curls and ringlets framing her face.

He straightened and met her at the bottom of the steps. She darned near took his breath away. "You look beautiful. I've got the belle of the ball tonight."

Cat blushed and gazed at him through her lashes. "You are so kind."

He offered his arm. "Shall we?"

Slipping her hand through, she smiled. "Of course." He tried to ignore how her touch coursed through his body as he helped her into the carriage and took the driver's seat. With a touch of the reins, the horse made a merry clip-clop down the street.

When they pulled up to the main entrance of the hall, where a clean walkway led inside, Jake told her, "I'll let you off here and hitch the horse to a post in the yard. I'll be right back."

She waited, and her lips curved at the corners as he offered his arm again. They entered into the lights and noise of many people enjoying the social evening. The gaslights in the chandeliers made everything sparkle, and the enticing aromas of food and refreshments wafted out into the lobby as the pair made their way to the hat check. Cat removed her cape, and Jake couldn't help an audible gasp. Over the bodice, creamy skin met his gaze, her bosom rising below. Her shoulders were bare, and a jewel-encrusted ribbon choker graced her neck. Jake worked to get his wits about him.

Inside the ballroom, the band started a waltz, and couples floated around the floor in their elegant attire. Jake turned to Cat. "Care to dance?"

She had a glint in her eye. "Delighted to."

At the edge of the dance floor, he put his hand on her back, she laid her fingers on his shoulder, and they whirled into the crowd. He was very aware of the way her body moved, and he kept his eyes firmly on her face.

At the end of the piece, Cat opened her fan. "My, it's warm in here."

Jake looked around and found an open table. "Sit here, and I'll get some refreshments. What would you like?"

"A small glass of port, please."

Jake moved through the tables and picked up two glasses of port and a plate of finger sandwiches. On his way back, he hesitated when he saw Albert Monroe with Cat. Plucking up his courage, he set the things on the table and turned to Albert. "Good evening, Mr. Monroe."

Albert straightened his spine. "I see you have taken my daughter out against my wishes."

"She's an adult, sir; she can decide for herself." Jake hovered over her protectively.

Cat cleared her throat. "I wish you two wouldn't

talk like I'm not here. That's impolite."

Albert glared at Jake. "Catherine, I want you to come and meet your brother John and his wife, Polly."

Cat rose, and Jake followed behind. John and Polly were several tables away. John eyed her when the introductions were made. "I remember you as a baby. You do remind me of Ma, though."

Polly nodded shyly, and Cat mentioned, "I saw you at church with your two children. They look delightful."

Polly blushed. "Thank you."

A dark form came sweeping in, and Jake was aware of the man's attention to Cat. Logan Henderson was one of the wealthiest men in the county, with the land that abutted the Bar Seven and Sugar Springs. He clasped Cat's hand. "Someone told me this enchanting creature was your daughter, Albert."

Albert looked less than pleased, but he made the introductions.

Henderson drew her hand to his lips. "Lovely to meet you, my dear. Welcome to Tombstone." He must have been feeding on grease, because he oozed manure. Jake ground his jaw. The band launched into another waltz. "Miss Monroe, will you honor me with this dance?"

Cat glanced at Jake and opened her mouth, then closed it again. "Yes."

Henderson whisked her off to the dance floor. Jake knew it was impolite for a woman to refuse a dance, but he wished she had.

John studied Jake closely as Albert went to the bar. "You seem to have a fixation on my sister. She came with you?"

"Your sister is a fascinating woman. Wait until you

get to know her. I befriended her when she first came to town, and I see her when I can."

Cat came back breathless and flushed. Henderson kissed her hand again. "Thank you, my dear, but I have to get back to my party." He disappeared into the crowd.

John looked around. "Seems like Pa got sidetracked at the bar. Why don't you two sit with us?"

Cat turned to Jake. "Could you retrieve our refreshments?"

"I'll be right back." Jake did her bidding and, when he returned, Cat and John were chatting. He slid into the available chair. "Are you sure your father won't mind me being here?"

John half-smiled. "Probably, but I don't think he'll do anything. I was telling Cat about the ranch." He turned to Cat. "Why don't you come to the ranch on Wednesday next, and I'll show you around? Pa usually goes into the back country to check on things that day."

She frowned. "I don't know. May Jake come with me?"

John hesitated. "I think I can call off the dogs, since he doesn't live at the Bar Seven anymore."

Jake smirked. "Now who's talking like I'm not here?"

Cat's eyes grew big. "I'm sorry. Could you escort me to Sugar Springs next Wednesday?"

"I think I can get some time off." He was already counting the days. The band started a polka, and he rose, bowing to Cat. "Before anyone else interrupts, may I have this dance?"

Cat laughed and reached for him. "Delighted to!"

They whirled onto the floor, and soon they were

flying to the lively beat. The room seemed to blur as he swung her around. When at last the music ceased, they were breathless and hanging onto each other.

Cat opened her fan. "My, I'm overheated now."

Jake held out his arm. "Want to step outside for a bit?" She slipped her hand through the crook of his elbow, and they went out the side door and to the back of the building. Strains of "Drink to Me Only With Thine Eyes" came floating into the night. The full Arizona moon made her creamy skin glow like alabaster. They did an impromptu slow waltz in the night air with some snorts and whinnying from the waiting horses. "Cat, you are so beautiful tonight."

She stopped, still in his arms, and raised her eyes to his face. He could feel her trembling beneath his touch as she said, "I'm beginning to feel more than friendship for you. Am I too bold to tell you this?"

Every nerve in his body came alert as tenderness and lust washed over him. "My dear sweet Miss Monroe, you don't know what joy it is to hear that confession." They stared transfixed at each other. Jake lightly caressed her cheek and moved his fingers to trace her neck to her shoulder. She seemed to soften as he hardened. Leaning down, his lips brushed hers lightly, and a small moan escaped her throat. His mouth sealed hers then, and he ran his tongue over her lips until she opened them and met him with a full kiss. Lord, she tasted sweet! He wanted her. Badly.

She pulled back and swallowed a couple of times. "Oh, Jake, that was"—she seemed to be searching for the right word—"breathtaking." She embraced him, fitting her body to his. "Let's do that again."

He leaned in for another kiss but was interrupted

by loud voices and a gunshot. Cat jumped back. Jake took her arm and guided her. "Stay behind me."

He peered around the corner of the building to where the noise was coming from. A crowd stood staring at two combatants—Albert Monroe and Stan Callahan. Callahan clung to one of the posts outside the hall. "You damned idiot! You could have killed me!"

Albert waved his gun. "Tell me you didn't put young Spencer up to this. You wanted to get a spy onto my ranch. I know you want to take this to court. I am not diverting water from your ranch!"

"I swear I didn't even know you had a daughter. I haven't seen the boy in over a year."

Jake moved between the two. "Mr. Monroe, nobody put me up to anything. I was attracted to your daughter before I knew who she was."

Albert swayed a little, and Jake suspected he was in his cups. "What are your intentions toward her?"

"I love her, sir."

Albert swung his fist and caught Jake on the side of the jaw. Stars exploded behind his eyes. "You mangy dog! What have you done to her?"

Cat pushed Albert back. "*Father*, Jake has been a perfect gentleman and a big help to me. Quit thinking the worst of him!"

Albert took a couple of steps back. "We'll speak of this another time." He turned to see John in the crowd behind him. "You and Polly get your things. We're leaving!"

Jake leaned against one of the posts, rubbing his cheek. *Good thing Albert is a little unsteady, or that hit could have been harder.* Cat came over and started fussing over him. He gently held her hand. "I'm all right. He didn't hit me that hard."

Her eyes clouded. "I wish he wasn't so mule-headed."

Mr. Callahan strode to them. "Miss Monroe, your father has always been that way. Once he has his mind set on something, it'll take an act of God to get him to change it."

She put her hands on her hips. "Mr. Callahan, why do you accuse my father of diverting the water?"

He frowned. "Because several times a year the arroyo dries up, but he seems to have water regardless."

"Couldn't it be something natural?"

He smirked. "That's the thing about you Monroes. I would think that, but it only started happening after Albert took over Sugar Springs." He turned on his heel and stalked back into the hall.

Jake held her gently by the shoulders. "Would you like to go?"

Cat opened her mouth as if to say something, then only nodded.

Jake turned. "I'll get our things. Wait here." He threaded his way through the milling people and retrieved his hat and coat and her cape from the hat check. Slipping the cape over her shoulders, he let his hands remain there for a moment before saying, "The rig is over there. I'll be right back." He drove the horse to the entrance and helped her up, then gathered the reins and hopped onto the driver's seat. "I'm sorry the evening had to end on such a sour note."

Her fingers lightly caressed his arm. "The trouble wasn't your fault. Most of the evening was enchanting. Thank you for taking me."

Warmth flushed through him, and he gave the whip

a snap. Shadow clip-clopped smartly down the street to the hotel. As he pulled up to the front door, he gazed at the beautiful woman beside him. "I truly wish that you lived by yourself."

Cat tried to frown, but it turned into a wide smile. "Why, Mr. Spencer, are you saying you want to take advantage of me?"

"Yes, Miss Monroe." Then he chuckled. "Am I being too bold?" He watched her studying him by the dim light coming from the door of the hotel.

The caress of her fingers on his face sent a tingle down to his groin. "I've never thought I'd long for intimacy with a man—until now."

Jake moaned and drew her over for a sweet, sweet kiss. When he finally pulled back, lightheaded, his only comment was, "You're a remarkable woman, Miss Monroe." Climbing down, he flipped the reins over the post, then helped Cat down and into his embrace. "I'll walk you to the lobby." She slipped her hand through his waiting arm. He couldn't help but thrill at her body moving so close to his. He removed his hat as they entered the hotel.

Cat stood in the yellow glow of the gaslights, and he gazed into her lash-shaded eyes. "Jake, I enjoyed the pleasure of your company tonight."

He cupped her face. "Thank you for accepting my invitation. I bid you a reluctant goodnight."

Shamelessly, she threw her arms around his neck and raised her face for an all-consuming kiss. "Goodnight." She started up the stairs, then turned. "Sleep well." An impish smile played over her lips, and she continued on her way.

Oh, that little coquette knows how to spin a web,

and I've become the willing fly. He spent a few moments to collect himself, then went to the carriage and returned it to the livery. Afterwards, in his room, he made his notes for the story to hand to Harvey on Monday.

Chapter 8

As Cat fixed her hat before going downstairs to meet Jake for the ride to Sugar Springs, she turned to Edna, who was mending a hem on one of her dresses. "Why don't you come with us to Sugar Springs? You need to get out once in a while."

Edna shook her head. "I'd feel like an intruder to you and Jake. I have a number of things here I have to do. Enjoy your trip."

Cat closed the door behind her and hurried to the stairs, pulling on her riding gloves as she descended. She smiled widely as she glimpsed Jake leaning against a post, waiting for her.

"Hello, sweetheart, you look wonderful today," he said as he straightened. "I saddled Mazie again for you."

"Thank you for escorting me again. I hope they won't object to you."

"John doesn't seem to mind. I can avoid your father."

Cat felt a streak of anger go through her. How could her father treat Jake so? "If he starts anything, we'll leave."

They went out to where the two horses waited in the warm sunshine. Cat scratched Mazie's nose, and the horse nickered. She gave her a sugar lump stashed in the pocket of her riding skirt, and Mazie happily crunched on it as Jake gave Cat a boost up and mounted his pinto. They threaded their way through the busy streets, then turned out of town.

The sun shone on the craggy hills around Tombstone. It was quite different from Virginia's green, rolling, fertile farmland. The grasses were interspersed with dry stretches of scrub brush and barren spots that were just rocky. She glanced at Jake, who looked deep in thought. He had been strangely quiet these past few days, like something was bothering him. "Jake, are you having second thoughts about escorting me to Sugar Springs?"

He eyed her, and an unconvincing smile crossed his face. "No. I was thinking how much more attractive you are without all that fabric and wire bouncing on your backside. Women are sure slaves to fashion."

She sniffed. "Usually it's men who come up with these designs, and if we don't fall into line, we're deemed social outcasts."

"We men can put on almost anything we please, and it doesn't change every season."

As one who tried to keep up with the latest style, it had never occurred to Cat to do anything else. "It's the way it's always been. I don't even know what clothes I would want, if I could choose."

Jake smirked. "That's what is meant by 'slave.' You have to be told."

This light banter on various topics continued until they reached the gate to Sugar Springs. They were half-way down the drive when a rider appeared from the trees by the hill. Cat shaded her eyes. "That looks like John."

John's horse galloped up to them. "I've had my

eyes out for you two. I wanted to warn you Pa is at the big house today with Logan Henderson. They've been powwowing about something all morning. You can follow me to my place."

He turned his horse and led the way. Instead of taking the left fork to the main building, they went to the right, down a long path that wound around a stand of cottonwoods. White puffs of seed floated on the breeze. In a grassy area on the shady side of the hill, Cat spotted a lovely small cabin. Morning glory vines crawled up one side, their deep purple flowers adding a splash of color to the wooden building.

Two children screeched out through the open door, and as soon as John dismounted, the boy and girl danced around his legs until he swept them up in his arms. After Cat slid to the ground, Jake walked the horses to the trough, and John brought the children over.

"Sam, Aggie, this is your Aunt Catherine." He set the children down and indicated with his hand. "Sam is four, and Aggie is two."

Cat squatted to their height and cupped their chins. "I'm very pleased to meet you. You can call me Aunt Cat."

They smiled shyly. Jake joined them, and John made the introductions. "This is your aunt's friend, Jake."

Sam studied him. "Are you our uncle?"

Cat's cheeks heated, and Jake laughed. "No—as of now."

Polly stepped out onto the cabin's wide front porch. She wore a brown work dress with a red apron. "I have a meal ready, if you would like to freshen up."

John showed them where the outhouse and pump were, and soon they sat in front of a delicious-smelling stew served with fresh baked bread and butter.

Cat admired the meal. "Polly, this is wonderful. You're an excellent cook."

Polly flushed. "I learned from my mother."

"Where are you from?"

"I met John in Tucson. My father runs a general store there."

Cat glanced at John. "You went all the way to Tucson for goods?"

John nodded. "This was six years ago, before Tombstone was built. We had to make a two-day trip for supplies back then."

Cat shook her head. "I forgot what a wilderness this must have been."

Jake put in, "Most of the towns outside of Tucson are just a few years old."

After the meal, John offered to take them on a tour of the ranch. After thanking Polly for the food, Cat, Jake, and John mounted their horses. Cat loved the rolling hills and the craggy mountains that dotted the landscape. John told them about the Sugar Springs that gave the ranch its name. A clear artesian spring that flowed out of the side of one of the mountains, it ran onto the meadows where the Monroes had their cattle. The brown-and-white Herefords contentedly munched on the grasses that were fed by the cold water.

"Would you like to see where Sugar Springs flows out?" John turned his horse toward a trail that wound into a canyon.

"Yes, I would." Cat and Jake had just turned their horses to follow when they heard a gunshot behind them.

All three whirled to find Ned Hadley riding up to them, gun drawn. "John, you know your father won't allow anyone from the Bar Seven to nose around our land!"

John glared. "Jake doesn't live there anymore!"

"That don't mean no never mind to your Pa. Jake's kin still lives there." He turned to Cat. "Anyway, I came to bring Miss Monroe back to the house."

Cat's stomach knotted. "Why?"

"Well, miss, I reckon that ain't any of my business. Just following orders."

Cat wavered between trying to get her father to like her and defense of Jake. Jake was far more helpful, but she had spent so long looking for her family, this was important to her, too. "I'll go see him."

John turned his horse around. "We'll all go back."

Jake set his jaw. Cat could see the muscles twitch. "Yes. I don't want to be called a spy."

The four rode to the house in silence. The tension speared the air around them like arrows. Jake gave her a hand off her horse and took both animals to the water trough. When Albert Monroe appeared at the door, his eyes went from one to another. "I want Catherine to come in. The rest of you wait on the porch."

In the sunny parlor, Cat found Logan Henderson sitting in one of the chairs. He rose with an expression like she'd seen on a tabby watching a goldfish. "Ah, the lovely Miss Monroe."

She nodded politely. "Mr. Henderson." She turned to Albert. "Is this something concerning him, as well?"

Albert glanced at Logan. "Yes, it is. Mr. Henderson came to ask me if he could pay court to you."

Cat pursed her lips. "Of course, you told him I've been seeing Mr. Spencer."

Albert paused. "No. I told him he may."

She sucked in a gasp. How dare he? "Father, may I see you in the hall? Excuse us, Mr. Henderson." She closed the door behind her. "How could you? I came to you because I wanted to find my family, and right away you start telling me who to see and what to do."

Albert took her by the shoulders. "Catherine, Logan is the richest man in the county and a neighbor of ours. You would want for nothing for the rest of your life. The Spencer boy owns no land, I'm sure he gets only a paltry sum working for the newspaper, and he's the son of the enemy."

Cat took a step back. "That's it, isn't it? You can't forgive his parentage. Well, we can't help where we're born. Tell Mr. Henderson I can't see him." She turned around and marched out the door.

"Catherine!" Her father followed her out, with Henderson behind him.

Cat grabbed Jake's arm and held him tight. She wasn't going to let her father take Jake from her.

Albert glared from one to the other, then went back and returned with a copy of a newspaper. He held it up in front of Cat. "Take a look at the recent *Epitaph*."

She set her jaw. "What am I looking for?"

"You'll know when you see it."

She glanced at Jake. Did she see a shadow of guilt in his eyes? Scanning the columns, she found one that read, "Long-lost daughter finds father. Our own Albert Monroe of Sugar Springs was found by his daughter, Catherine Monroe." She went on to read her personal story, one that only Jake would know. Humiliation swelled in her breast. She shook the paper in Jake's face. "What's the meaning of this? Am I just an assignment for you? How dare you use me like this!"

Jake flushed. "Wait! Let me explain! Yes, you started out as an assignment, but things changed. My editor still wanted me to do the story since I had all the notes."

"Why didn't you tell me? I thought you were doing all this out of the goodness of your heart."

His eyes pleaded with her. "I'm sorry, Cat, I should have told you. I didn't count on falling in love with you."

"Go, Jake. Take Mazie and leave. I won't be going back with you."

"But—" He grasped her hand.

Wrenching it free, she ran into the house, her eyes filling with tears. "Leave me alone!" She collapsed on a sofa and sobbed.

Henderson came in and stood in front of her. "Miss Monroe, I want you to know there is someone who cares about you. I'll go now, but I'll be back tomorrow."

After Henderson left, Albert came in and sat beside her. "I told John to take the carriage and pick up your maid and baggage from the hotel. The housekeeper is fixing up a couple of bedrooms for the both of you."

Cat nodded. "Thank you, Father." Still stunned, she rested her head on the back of the sofa and closed her eyes.

Was she too hasty? She thought of Jake, and there was still love there, but he had betrayed her.

On the other hand, her father wanted Henderson to court her. He had to be nearing forty, but he had money.

She shook her head. She felt nothing for him.

As she gazed out the window, melancholy overtook her.

Chapter 9

The Bird Cage's gambling parlor was a noisy din as Jake looked up from the faro game. "Well," growled a cowpoke across the table, "you gonna play?"

The cigar smoke hung in foggy threads around the room. Jake rose unsteadily to his feet and gathered his chips. "Naw, I'm out this turn." He swayed to the bar. "Hey, barkeep, another shot." His nickel hopped on the polished wood. Glass in hand, he threw back the shot and almost continued to the floor. Someone slipped in beside him.

"Hey, honey, take it easy on that stuff."

He turned to see a blurry Dara with a hand on his shoulder. "Pfft, I can handle it. What are you doin' here? You run out of customers?"

She took his arm. "Come on. Let's get some air." When they reached the front entrance, she sat him down on the bench out front. "Darlin', you want to tell Dara what's got your knickers in a knot?"

He gazed at her. "She tole me to take Mazie and go. Jus' like that. 'Cause I wrote that story about her." He hiccupped.

"Miss Monroe booted you out, huh? Can you make it back to your room?"

"Um—"

Dara hauled him up and, with surprising strength, guided him a block and a half to his walk-up.

Amazingly, she got him up the stairs without losing him, although a couple of times he almost went over the rail. Inside the room, she leaned him against the wall and removed his holster and outer clothing. She snorted. "I don't usually do this without money." With a little leverage, she rolled him into bed. That's when he lost consciousness.

The sun hit him in the eyes when he came to. He was frozen in place like a dead man. Turning to check the clock on the table next to the bed, he found he'd made a serious mistake. He grabbed the chamber pot from under the bed and was wracked with heaves for the next minute or so. Maybe he could roll over and die. His head felt like it was split down the middle. He sank into blackness again.

A pounding on the door woke him again. "Jake! Are you there? It's Daniel!"

It took a second to get his wits about him. "I'm here. Come in," he called weakly.

When Daniel came in, he made a face. "It smells like unholy hell in here." He opened the two windows. "Dara asked me to check on you. She said you pickled yourself pretty good last night."

Jake pointed a shaky finger to a cloth on the washstand. "Wet that down with water…give it to me."

Daniel poured some of the water from the pitcher into the basin and submerged the cloth. When it was thoroughly saturated, he handed it to Jake, who bathed his whole head. The combination of the water and the breeze from the window revived him somewhat. Daniel sat on one of the chairs. "Dara told me Cat was angry about the story you put in the paper."

Jake was silent for a moment. "I shouldn't have

done that story. She felt betrayed."

"Apologize to her."

"I did. She didn't accept."

"Give her time to cool off; then talk to her."

"That won't be easy. She's staying at the ranch, and Henderson is paying court."

Daniel stood. "You'll think of something. I've got to get back to work." He let himself out.

Jake stayed and pondered for a few minutes. Daniel was right; he'd think of something. He tried to get up, but his head throbbed. Reclining again, he figured it could wait for a while.

****

Cat gazed out the window of her bedroom as she repaired the lace on one of her dresses. The ranch was beautiful, with its rolling hills at the foot of a chain of mountains, the green grass near the spring water interspersed with desert plants and cacti in the dry areas. Her reverie was interrupted by a knock at the door. "Yes?"

"It's Edna. May I speak with you?"

"Of course! Come in." Cat set her sewing down.

Edna sat on a chair across from Cat. She started to fidget, pulling at her fingers. "Miss Catherine, I've been with you since you were a child. You're a grown woman now, living with your family. They have a housekeeper and a maid—"

"Edna! What are you trying to say?"

Edna smoothed back an imaginary wisp of hair out of her eyes. "Well, I'd like to leave your employ."

Cat stared stupidly at her. "Is it something I've done or said?"

Edna blushed. "Oh, my, no. It's just that I have a

beau in town whom I want to marry."

Cat's mouth wouldn't close for a few moments. "When did this happen?"

"When you and Jake were out, I became friends with Ed."

"Ed?"

"The desk clerk at the Grand. Ed Matthews." She picked at her sleeve. "We were thinking about going to the justice of the peace, since neither of us have family."

A wave of sadness swept over Cat. "I've always thought of you like a mother since mine died so soon after I was born. You've taken care of me for so long, starting when I was six…"

Edna's eyes teared up and she sniffed into her handkerchief. "Now you're nineteen and don't need me to look after you. This is hard for me, too. I'm thirty-five, and I find I want a life for myself." She grasped Cat's hand. "I want you to be my witness."

"Of course I will. Do you know when?"

"We haven't set a date yet, but I'll let you know. I'm moving back to town today." She hesitated for a moment. "I have to tell you something before I go, but it's breaking a promise I made."

"What is it?"

Edna took a breath. "I knew your aunt told your father you died."

Cat tried to speak but couldn't for a second. "Why did she do it?"

"You have to understand—she had grown so fond of you by then, and she didn't want to give you up. So when your father wrote that letter, she suspected he wouldn't come back to stay in Virginia but would take you away, so she told him you were dead." Edna flushed. "I accidentally overheard her speaking to your uncle, and she made me promise I would never tell you. I should have told you when you received the letter from your father. I'm so sorry."

Cat rose and pulled Edna up with her. "I forgive you. You were doing what you thought best at the time. It's not true you don't have family. We'll always be yours."

Edna embraced her. "Thank you. That means a lot to me." Edna left, and Cat sank into melancholy. Things had fallen apart since she left Virginia. Yes, she had completed her quest to find her family, but her father was out to get her married off as soon as he could. Did that mean he saw her as an inconvenience? And to Henderson, a man who had to be twenty years her senior, not to the man she truly loved—Jake.

She picked up her needlework and put it down again. She couldn't see through the tears that glazed her sight. Maybe she should have listened to what Jake had to say. But Father was dead set against her having anything to do with him. What next?

A knock broke into her thoughts, and the maid, Nell, opened the door. "Miss Catherine? Your father requests your presence at midday meal. Shall I say you will be down?"

She dried her eyes with her handkerchief and stood. "Tell him I'll be down in a couple of minutes." Nell nodded and left.

Cat washed her face and hands at the washstand. She glanced at the mirror and pinched her cheeks to get some color in them. Then she hurried down and found the place that was set at the table for her.

Albert looked up as she came into the dining room. "Why have you spent the morning in your room?"

"I had some sewing to do, and I wanted to settle in. Did Edna leave?"

"Mr. Matthews was here just after she went to see you. They left a few minutes ago. She told me about your aunt and the letter."

"Auntie must have really wanted me to stay, for her to do such a horrible thing."

Albert waved her off. "What's done is done. Now I know."

The housekeeper came in with two plates of sliced beef, fried potatoes, and gravy over all. Fresh bread and butter were on smaller plates in front of them. Cat took a sip of water before digging in.

Albert paused and set down his knife. "I got a message from Logan that he wants to stop by this afternoon and show you around his ranch."

Cat felt a weight in the pit of her stomach. "He doesn't waste any time, does he?"

"Give him a chance, Cat. I know he's older than you, but he's settled and rich. A merging of our two ranches would bring in more money for both of us."

Cat pursed her lips. "In other words, this is a business deal."

"Honey, I'm just pointing out the advantages."

She made a slight grunt, then went on, "Papa, could you tell me why you're so hard on Daniel? He told me his side of the story. I'd like to hear yours."

He scowled, but said, "He was lazy and couldn't take orders. After several mishaps with the stock, he packed his bags and left. Things have gone smoother since he vamoosed."

She shook her head. "Maybe he wasn't cut out for ranching. It must be hard work down in the mine."

"Is that what he's doing now?"

"You didn't know?"

He picked his meat with his fork. "We haven't exactly been on speaking terms."

"He really is a nice person." She finished her meal and wiped her mouth with the napkin. "Since I'm going out this afternoon, may I be excused to change clothes?"

Albert nodded and seemed to be lost in thought. She rose and went to her room to get ready for an outing she wasn't looking forward to.

Nell came up an hour later and announced, "Mr. Henderson is here to see you."

Cat put her sewing down. "Tell him I'll be down." Nell left, and Cat rose and checked herself in the mirror. She pinned her veiled hat on her head and slipped on her gloves.

Half way down the stairs, she heard her father saying, "I'm not going to do that."

Henderson's voice rang clear. "Albert, women need guidance. They can't make important decisions on their own."

Cat stood in the doorway, her lips pressed together. "This courtship is not starting well."

Henderson whirled to face her and smiled. "Surely, you didn't think I meant all women."

Her father shook his head. "You'd better leave before you step in another pile."

Henderson extended his hand to Cat. "Shall we go?"

She ignored it and took her parasol off the hook by

the door. "Whenever you're ready."

Henderson glanced at Albert and opened the front door, and Cat sashayed out ahead of him, walking to the waiting carriage. Henderson gave her help getting in, then went around and gathered the reins. With a smart slap of the driving whip, they were off.

Cat opened her parasol to shield her complexion from the midday sun. Henderson glanced at her. "I'm sorry you heard what you did. I didn't mean what I said."

"Are you in a habit of saying things you don't mean?"

He reined in the horse and turned to her. "Let's start from here and consider what you heard was a mistake. I would like to know you better, so you can set me straight on my wrong thinking. Deal?"

She paused, then said, "Deal."

Ten minutes later, they turned on a wide drive going into a patch of cottonwood trees. The end of the drive was graced by a large dusky-blue Queen Anne house with a wide porch. Large field stones made a substantial foundation.

Cat marveled at the handsome residence. "What a lovely house!"

Henderson climbed down from the driver's seat and helped her out. "I had a builder come in from San Francisco ten years ago. Come inside."

As they walked up the steps, the front door opened and a distinguished-looking gray-haired black man stood there. "Welcome home, Mr. Henderson." He stepped back as they entered the home.

Henderson gave his hat to the man. "Could you take Miss Monroe's things and then bring some lemonade and ice into the parlor?"

He inclined his head. "Yes, sir."

Henderson led Cat into the lavishly furnished parlor and waved his hand toward a dark blue velvet couch. "Sit. Make yourself comfortable." The breeze from the bright open windows billowed the expensive lace curtains.

Cat looked around at the fine art and figurines. "For being a bachelor, you have taste."

He grew quiet, then shook his head. "My late wife, Hallie, decorated the house."

"Oh, I'm sorry. I didn't know you were married before."

"She died six years ago."

The butler brought in the refreshments, set them on the serving table, and poured the lemonade into the tall glasses. "Anything else, sir?"

Henderson gave one of the glasses to Cat. "No, Bill. You may go." The butler backed out of the room.

Cat took a sip of the sweet-tart liquid before turning to Henderson. "Illness?"

"Excuse me?"

"Did she die of an illness?"

"Oh—yes. Let's go on to happier topics." He smiled at her.

She smiled back, but made an observation. *He smiles, but it doesn't reach his eyes. They look cold, like there is no warmth in him.* As they chatted, her thoughts kept turning to Jake. She couldn't help it. She missed him.

Chapter 10

Jake stared at the empty sheet of paper on his desk. The throbbing in his head had turned into a dull nagging ache, but he still couldn't concentrate on his job. He put his elbows on the paper and his head in his hands, a vision of despair. A sharp rap on the desktop made him jump.

Harvey glared down at him. "I know you took yesterday off 'cause you were—sick, but we need reporters here, not paperweights."

Jake stared back at him, then turned in his chair and rose. "I'll go on my rounds. I need some fresh air anyway." He grabbed his coat and hat and pushed the door open. As he stepped out into the sunlight, a gnawing sensation grabbed at his gut. There was something about Henderson that bothered him, and not because he was courting Cat. He remembered the death of Henderson's wife had caused tongues to wag some, locally. There was no undertaker or lawman around before the town was built, so no inquiry was ever made. She was buried on the ranch property, and that was that.

He slid through the door of the Bird Cage and found Dara at a table with a mug of coffee. She glanced up and grinned. "Well, Jake, you look like hell this morning."

"Feel like it, too." He lowered himself into the seat across from her. "Is there any more coffee in the place?"

She rose and sauntered over to the bar, where she picked up a cup and towel before heading to the stove to pour the steaming black liquid into the mug. Tossing the towel back onto the bar, she set the coffee in front of Jake. "Five cents, please."

He flipped a nickel onto the table. "Got time to talk?"

"What do you want?"

"What have you heard about Logan Henderson?"

A quick shadow passed over her face. She shrugged. "Pretty much what everyone else has. He's rich, but doesn't socialize, as far as I know."

"What about the death of his wife?" Did he detect a slight flinch?

"Nothing, really. I lived in Tucson before I came here, and not much news traveled north."

"Who might know?"

She was silent for a bit. "Your ma might know. After all, she lives nearby, and women have a pipeline into family information."

Jake dreaded the thought of having to go to Callahan's, but Dara was right. He rose and flipped another nickel onto the table. "Thanks. I'll see her."

She pocketed the two nickels. "You're welcome, handsome."

He strode to the livery stable and saddled up his horse. *Why am I doing this? Cat made it clear to me she didn't want to see me again. Guilt?* He rode out of town wondering what on earth he was going to say to his mother and hoping to hell he didn't run into his father.

****

Cat studied her reflection in the vanity mirror while

she brushed her hair. *What is wrong with you? You're letting your father dictate your life. Where is your spine? He hardly knows you.* She set her brush down. *I have to talk to my father.* A rap sounded on her door. "Yes?"

"Breakfast is ready, Miss Catherine," said Nell.

Cat opened the door. "Tell my father I'll be down in a few minutes."

Nell gave a short curtsy. "Yes, miss."

Cat took one of the ribbons lying on her dresser and tied her hair back, then began pacing the floor and wringing her hands. *Should I tell him I don't want anything to do with Henderson?* She heaved a sigh and went downstairs. Her father wasn't in the dining room yet, so she stood behind her chair at the table.

Albert bustled in. "Sit. We don't stand on ceremony here." He plopped onto his chair just as she slid into hers.

Nell brought in the griddlecakes and sausage, set them on the table, and went back into the kitchen for the warm maple syrup and coffee. When they had been placed in front of Albert, she asked, "Anything else, sir?"

Albert shook his head. "No." As Nell left, he turned to Cat. "Well, how did you get along with Logan yesterday?"

She picked at her sausage with the fork. "It was— interesting."

"Interesting. What kind of an answer is that? This is the man who wants to court you."

"Father, he's as cold as a tongue sandwich. His smile never reaches his eyes."

Albert scowled. "He also has enough money to

keep you in the way you are accustomed."

Cat glared at him. "I don't love him. I'd be able to live with less."

Albert silently ate for a few minutes. "I know I had to work hard to prove to your mother's parents that I was worthy to take care of her."

"Father, times are changing. I can take care of myself. I proved that when I came searching for you. I have a feeling Logan Henderson could be a very cruel man if he wanted to be, and I wouldn't like to be on the receiving end of that cruelty." She felt a plea in her voice.

"Give him a chance. You hardly know him." Cat opened her mouth to speak, but he waved her off. "I don't want to hear another word."

She picked at her food for a few more moments, then stood. "Excuse me, please. I'm not hungry. I'm going for a walk." She made her way to the porch and took a deep breath. Then she headed down the path to John and Polly's cabin. The children were on the porch, Sam shelling peas and Aggie dragging her doll around by the foot. Sam looked up and yelled, "Auntie!" and as he did, the bowl turned over in the dirt with a clatter. Peas went rolling out everywhere like little marbles.

Polly came out to see what was going on and exclaimed, "Sam, what have you done?"

Cat, in an effort to help, scooped up peas by the handfuls. "Don't be hard on him. Most of these look all right. Just need to be rinsed."

After they had set things right, Sam continued his job and Polly turned to Cat. "Did you want something?"

Cat sighed. "I'd like to talk, if you have a few minutes."

"Come in for a cup of coffee. I have a pot on the back burner." Polly waved her into the small kitchen and pulled out a chair at the table. "I'm making elderberry jam for the winter and have some jelly glasses sterilizing on the stove, but there's still room for the coffeepot."

Polly poured a cup for Cat in a ceramic mug and set cream and sugar in front of her. Then she took the pot of jam and started ladling it into the steaming glasses.

Cat gestured. "Let me have the wax and I'll seal them for you." She set at her task. "Polly, you know Father better than I. Is he always hard to reason with?"

Polly hesitated. "I've always found him reasonable, but it's hard to change his mind once he sets it."

Cat sighed. "That's what I was afraid of."

"Does this have to do with Mr. Henderson? John told me what happened."

Cat nodded. "I'm having second thoughts about sending Jake away. I still care for him. And deep down, something about Henderson bothers me."

Polly sucked on her lower lip. "I know girls are raised to respect their elders' wishes, but people can be very wrong at times."

"I wish I could put my finger on what bothers me about him, but I can't."

They finished their task, and Cat turned to Polly as she readied to leave. "Thank you for listening to me. I guess I have to work this out myself."

She waved to the children on the way out and started up the path to the house. As she came around the bend, she balked. Henderson's carriage was in the yard.

****

Jake wiped his face with his handkerchief and gazed at the big Callahan house. Callahan never had married, so Jake's family was in charge of taking care of things when he was working away from the ranch house. He looked around hoping he wouldn't see his father's horse. It wasn't in evidence anywhere so far. Riding to the back, he spotted his mother dumping a basin of dirty water off the porch.

She looked up at the sound of hooves and moved stray hairs out of her eyes. Joy radiated from her face. "Jake! You've come back!" She set the basin on a chair and hurried down the steps as he dismounted.

He caught her in an embrace. "Not to stay, but it's good to see you, Ma!" A few more lines in her face and a few more streaks of silver in her hair, but she was still a good-looking woman. "Is Pa anywhere around?"

"He's with Mr. Callahan, checking the herd. There might be a mountain lion lurking around. We lost one of our calves yesterday." She motioned toward the house. "Come in for some coffee and talk. We need to catch up." She picked up the basin, and Jake followed her inside.

He hung his hat on one of the pegs next to the door and sat on a chair next to the table, while his mother poured the fragrant liquid into a mug.

"Do you want anything to eat?"

"No, Ma, I'm not real hungry."

"You look a little pale. Are you all right?"

He shook his head. "Just tired. Ma, I came to ask you about Hallie Henderson. How well did you know her?"

She sat in the chair across from him and began to peel potatoes. "If I remember correctly, she was always sickly, from the moment she and her husband moved here. It wasn't long after they were married in Texas. I talked to her a few times, but she didn't go out socially."

"Did he always have the ranch land that he has now?"

"Oh, my, no. That was her family's land. The Buckleys had the land here and some in Texas. Her pa was a speculator who bought land in several states and territories. I believe he gave them this land for a wedding present."

Something was screaming in the back of Jake's mind, but he couldn't put it together yet. A strong fear for Cat wormed into his gut. "Has he seen any woman socially since his wife died?"

She thought for a moment, then shook her head. "None that I know of. Everyone was surprised when he showed up for that ball in town, the most recent one. He usually doesn't go in for dancing."

They continued talking about mundane things, but Jake was putting together a not-too-pretty picture of Henderson. Did Henderson want to sink his teeth into some of the Monroe land? And how opportune that a Monroe daughter showed up when she did.

"You're interested in that Monroe girl, aren't you?"

He gave his mother a jaw drop but recovered quickly. "What made you ask that?"

"All these questions about Logan and Hallie. You were never interested in the Hendersons until Miss Monroe came to town. Your pa told me you were seeing her." She pursed her lips. "You could make an enemy if you keep it up. Henderson doesn't suffer fools lightly."

"I wouldn't worry too much about that. Cat and I

had a bit of a misunderstanding, and we parted." Guilt gave him a bit of a wallop again.

She looked him in the eyes. "You don't like him paying court to her, though."

He ground his back teeth. "No, I don't." He rose. "I have to be getting back to town. Thanks for the coffee and the conversation."

"Oh, I nearly forgot. Peggy is getting into town today on the noon stage. Could you meet her?"

Taking his hat from the hook, he nodded. "Sure will."

She came over and hugged him. "Just be careful, Jake. You're the only son I have left."

"I will, Ma." He kissed the top of her head and strode out the door. Shoving his hat on, he took a quick glance around to see if his pa was anywhere in sight, then mounted his horse and headed back.

Chapter 11

Cat closed her eyes for a few moments before going into the house. She didn't want to deal with Henderson, but she had no choice. A blue jay landed and scolded in a cottonwood, while the carriage horse snorted, being disturbed. The mid-October temperatures were warmer than she was used to, and beads of moisture popped out on her upper lip. She pulled her handkerchief out and dabbed at it. *May as well face them.* She straightened her spine and went inside.

"Ah, here she is now. Cat, come into the parlor," she heard her father say.

"Said the spider to the fly," she mumbled under her breath.

Her father stood by the fireplace, and Henderson was poised on the couch like he was ready to run. "Logan thinks you should put your inheritance in a bank, and I agree."

With an evil-eye side glance at Henderson, she said, "You know I have to have a cosigner for that."

"Logan has volunteered."

"No," fell out of her mouth without a thought.

Henderson gave her a cold stare. "I'm your intended."

"If it's all the same to you, I'd rather have my father cosign." She stared pointedly at Albert. "Logan Henderson has never proposed marriage to me. We've only had one outing."

Henderson made a low noise in his throat.

Albert shuffled his feet and wiped his hand across his mouth. "I'll cosign. But if you marry Logan, it'll transfer to him."

Not in a million years. Cat huffed. "When do you want to do this?"

Albert gave Henderson a sideways glance. "Logan was going to take you today, but we all can go. It may be better to have more protection, with all that money." He pulled a strongbox off the shelf. "Put your bank notes in here, and we can put it under the seat."

Henderson rose. "I'll help you."

Cat shook her head. "I'm perfectly capable of loading it myself. Anyway, you shouldn't be in a lady's boudoir." She turned on her heel and stalked out.

The late morning sun's rays highlighted floating dust specks, and they danced as she swept by them. Pulling the trunk from the wall, she carefully pressed a hidden latch and removed the false bottom. Stacks of bank notes, totaling a little less than three thousand dollars, lay tucked in the secret chamber. She transferred them to her father's strongbox and turned the key. The key was popped into her reticule, and she grabbed her parasol on the way out.

Henderson made a move to take the box, but she pulled back. "I'll feel better if I take it out."

At the carriage, Henderson sharply turned. "I'll bolt it under the seat, if it meets with your approval, madam."

After that was done, Cat sat sandwiched between her father and Henderson. Henderson gave a smart crack with the whip, and they were off on a silent trip into town. A stagecoach clattered past as they pulled in next to the bank, and Henderson unbolted the strongbox. She glanced across the street, and her heart sank to her shoes. Jake was hugging a young lady. Cat's vision blurred. *No. I'm not going to cry. But it didn't take him very long to latch onto another girl.* She sniffed as she turned and followed the men into the bank.

Her father went to a teller's cage and set the box down, and the young man behind the grille nodded. "Mr. Monroe, may I be of assistance?"

"Yes, Ted, my daughter wants to open an account here."

The young man gave a slight nod in her direction. "Ah, yes, Miss Catherine Monroe. I'll tell Mr. Billings."

They were led to an office, and an older gentleman with hard gray eyes motioned to a couple of chairs. "Please be seated."

Henderson stood by the door, and Cat wished he had stayed outside, but her father and Mr. Billings didn't say anything. Her father pushed the box toward the banker. "This is the money Cat brought with her when she came to town."

Billings opened it and started counting the bank notes. "You have two thousand, eight hundred, fifty-six dollars. These notes are from the Bank of Virginia. They aren't old Confederate bills, are they?"

She shook her head. "No, sir. If you look at the date, they were issued only two years ago."

He closely inspected the piece of paper, then nodded. "It looks authentic. Since your father and Mr. Henderson seem to believe you, I will, too." He opened a drawer and pulled out a form. "Who will cosign for you?"

"My father will."

He filled out the paper and put check marks where she and her father were to sign. When that was done, they all rose, and Billings put out his hand. "Welcome to the Bank of Tombstone, Miss Monroe."

His handshake was a firm grip, and he shook her father's hand, as well. As they exited the bank, Cat glanced in the direction of the stagecoach stop, where she had seen Jake, but he wasn't there. Part of her was disappointed.

"Shall we go to lunch while we're here?" Henderson inquired with a wave of his hand to the restaurant next door.

Cat wasn't hungry, but she followed anyway.

****

Jake had spotted Peggy stepping off the stage and waved. She returned the wave and hurried to meet him as the driver hauled down her trunk and put it on the wooden walk. The stage took off again, and Jake led Peggy to the walk. "It's good to see you again, Sis. Welcome home." He gave her a hug. "How is Auntie?"

"Back to her old cranky self. The ague was bad this time." She motioned toward the trunk. "Can you hire a rig to take this back to the ranch? Pa brought it out when I left, so maybe I can hitch Mazie to the back of the rig, and you can return it to town for me."

Jake had visions of running into his father this time, but what the hell. Maybe he wouldn't say anything in front of Peggy. "Would you like something to eat first? We can stop in across the street."

"I am a bit parched after the stagecoach ride. But

where should we stash the trunk?"

Jake thought for a moment. "We can hire a rig and bolt your trunk under the seat, then hitch up the rig here while we eat." They picked up the trunk between them and headed toward the livery stable. While the rig was being readied, Jake saddled Mazie and secured her reins to the back of the rig. He helped Peggy up and swung in on the driver's side, and they rode back down the street.

At the door of the restaurant, Jake opened it for his sister and followed her into the dining room, which was cooled by a battery fan. He jolted when he spotted Cat with Albert and Henderson. She was sitting with her back toward him. He stopped Peggy with a hand on her shoulder. "Maybe we could go to another restaurant. There's an ice cream parlor down the street."

Peggy turned. "What's the matter? You look ashen."

Just then Cat looked around, and a stricken shadow crossed her face. She rose from the table with an "Excuse me." Hurrying toward the door, she paused as Jake stepped in front of her.

"Cat, wait—"

Her face showed hurt and anger as she shoved past him. Albert and Henderson got up from the table, and Henderson cornered Jake as Albert went out after Cat. "You stay away from her, you hear?"

Jake balled his fists. "You have no say over her, Henderson. Or over me, either."

Henderson was practically nose to nose with him. "We'll see about that, Spencer."

Jake aimed a roundhouse at Henderson's jaw, and the man crashed into a nearby table. Henderson came at Jake and knocked him down. Both were on the floor trading blows when a big burly cook came out from the back of the restaurant. "What the hell is going on here?" He grabbed Henderson, and Peggy held Jake.

Henderson shook off the man's grip and straightened his coat. "Just a difference of opinion." He glared at Jake. "This isn't finished." He stalked out the door.

Peggy dusted off Jake. "What was that all about?" She took her handkerchief and blotted some blood from his mouth.

Jake picked up his hat and tipped it to the cook. "Don't worry, I'm leaving." Pulling some silver dollars out of his vest pocket, Jake handed them to the cook. "This should take care of any damage." He steered Peggy out the door. "Let's go to the ice cream parlor. I have a long and complicated story to tell you." She glanced at him briefly, then followed.

****

Pressed between her father and Henderson, Cat spoke not a word all the way back to the ranch. She seethed to the boiling point. All she had hoped for, making up with Jake, had gone out the window in one fell swoop. When Henderson moved to help her out of the carriage, she pulled back sharply. "Don't touch me!" She hopped down on her own and strode into the house and up the stairs. From her window she observed Henderson and her father engaged in an animated conversation. Henderson snapped the buggy whip a couple of times against his boot, then climbed into the driver's seat and drove off. Her father turned toward the house.

She heard her father's tread on the stairs and a light tapping on the door. "Cat. May I come in?"

"Yes."

He regarded her with pursed lips. "You weren't very polite to Logan. Even after he saved you from that vile Spencer."

She tapped her foot. "Father, I didn't need to be saved from Jake. He made no move against me. I just wish Mr. Henderson would stay out of my business."

"Didn't they teach you manners on how to behave when you're being courted?"

"Jake was treating me better than that. So far, all Henderson has done is discuss business and try to get hold of my money. I don't trust him."

Her father shook his head. "He's been my friend for years. You're not being fair to him. The masquerade ball is coming up in two weeks. I'll get tickets for all of us. Promise me you'll have him as an escort. If you still feel that way, I'll talk to him." He waited a moment, and when she didn't reply he turned and left.

Cat sat on her bed hugging her pillow. *Why, oh, why, is he pressing this issue? He barely knows me, but he wants to marry me off to this friend of his. What have I gotten myself into?* She couldn't help it; she still longed for Jake.

****

Jake shifted on the rig's seat and glanced at Peggy, who was studying him. "I must say, big brother, you really stepped in some wet cow chips this time. Most people wouldn't dare cross Henderson."

"Can't help it. I can't get over Cat, but I keep doing foolish things."

"Isn't the masquerade ball in a couple of weeks? I know the Monroes usually go to the social dances."

"How is that going to help?" He stared out ahead.

97

"You can apologize to her and tell her how you feel. You tell me you can't get over her, but does she know?" He glanced at her, and she had a smug expression.

"You know how our parents feel about the Monroes."

She wrinkled her nose. "Oh, honestly, she wasn't responsible for the blowup about the water, and besides, nothing has ever been proved." She smiled. "And things might cool down if you married her."

"Or get worse," he said with a twitch on the reins that lightly slapped the horse's backside and quickened the pace.

"You can escort me to the ball. With a mask on, you can approach her and ask for a dance. Then you can talk to her."

He shook his head. "You have this all figured out, don't you, Miss Cupid."

She grinned. "Yep."

Callahan's ranch was coming into view, and Jake concentrated on the clip-clop of the carriage horse and of Mazie, who was tied behind. The mid-afternoon sun cast puzzle pictures on the craggy hills in front of them. He scanned the paddock inside the gate and noticed his father's roan stallion. *I'm riding into the valley of the shadow of death.*

He turned the horse through the gate and pulled up by the back door as their parents came out to greet Peggy. He hauled her trunk to the porch, untied Mazie's reins, and had picked up the saddle and blanket and begun leading her to the paddock when he heard his father call.

"Hey, boy, I heard you and that Monroe girl had a

fight." He caught up with Jake and walked beside him.

Jake looked at the ground as he set the saddle down. "She does have a name. Her name is Cat—Catherine."

"Well, it's all for the best. You wouldn't want to be tied up with those Monroes. Damn rebs."

Jake unbuckled the reins and opened the gate to the paddock. "I thought the war was over years ago." He slapped Mazie's rump, and the horse trotted inside as he closed it again. He glanced at his father. "Albert can be stubborn as a jackass, but the family isn't as bad as you think."

His father frowned. "Think on what I said before. Stay away from her." He turned and went to the house.

Jake hefted the saddle and blanket over his shoulder and took it into the stable. "I'll give it all the thought it deserves, Pa," he said under his breath.

Chapter 12

Cat had accidentally stepped on and torn the bottom ruffle of one of her petticoats. She was mending it when there was a knock at her door. "Yes?"

"May I come in?" her father asked.

"I'm decent."

The door opened, and he stood in front of her. "We're invited for dinner at Logan's house tonight."

"We?"

"You, me, John, and Polly."

"Why?"

He scowled. "Do you have to be suspicious about everything? It's a friendly gesture to all of us."

"Father, you just can't seem to see that man is up to something. I don't trust him. Especially not after he tried to cosign my bank deposit."

He sighed. "Be ready by four." He turned and left.

She glanced at her mantel clock. It was two forty-seven. She finished her stitching, folded the petticoat, and found herself mindlessly pacing the floor and wringing her hands. *I thought I could find peace when I found my father, but it seems I only complicated my life.* She removed her dinner dress from the wardrobe and shook it out. She had last worn it when she was with Jake.

When she joined her father downstairs, John and Polly were just arriving with the children, and she greeted them warmly. Sam and Aggie were going to be cared for by Nell while their parents were away. Polly glanced at Cat with concern, but she didn't say anything.

Albert put on his hat. "Let's go. I have the carriage ready."

The afternoon sun stretched the shadows of the trees into long stripes. They talked about mundane things on the fifteen-minute trip to the Henderson ranch, while the clip-clopping of the horses marked a cheery beat that Cat was far from feeling.

Bill, Henderson's butler, met them at the door and escorted them into the parlor. He took their wraps and the men's hats and then departed. Henderson rose from his desk in the corner of the room. "Please be seated. Dinner should be ready in a half hour. Would you like something to drink before then? Sherry?"

Cat, Albert, and John nodded. Polly spoke meekly, "I'm temperate. I'll have water, if you please."

"As you wish, Mrs. Monroe." He rang for Bill, who appeared promptly. "Get four sherries and a water."

Bill inclined his head. "Yes, sir." When Bill returned, he set the tray of cut-crystal stem glasses down and retreated from the room.

Henderson passed the glasses around and raised his high. "Here's to dear neighbors. May we stay close."

Cat gave a small flinch before she took a sip. Henderson, John, and her father went into a conversation on the ranching business. Polly sidled over and sat next to Cat.

"Did you talk to Father about how you feel?" Polly asked, low.

Cat blew out a breath. "You were right. It's hard to change his mind about anything." She paused to make sure the men weren't paying attention. "In town, I saw Jake with another woman."

Polly frowned. "Are you sure she wasn't just a friend of his?"

She related to Polly what had happened at the restaurant. "Henderson came out looking disheveled and told me never to speak of Jake again. I think they got into a fight."

Just then Bill came in and announced that dinner was ready. As she suspected, Henderson had arranged for her to be next to him, and Polly was on the other side of the table. They were served a tomato soup and crusty bread to begin with, and Henderson stood to say grace. After the "Amen," he raised his glass of wine. "I want to announce my engagement to the lovely Miss Monroe."

Cat's soup spoon clattered to the bowl. "Mr. Henderson! You haven't even asked me!"

The corners of his mouth edged up into a sinister smile. "No need, my dear. Your father has already given permission." Polly gasped.

Cat rose and stamped her foot. "What on earth possessed you?" she directed at both Henderson and her father. She picked up her soup and flung it at Henderson, leaving a splatter of red on his elegant white shirt. Running out of the dining room, she collided with Bill.

"Leave Tombstone and never come back," he said softly, so only she could hear.

She burst out the front door and ran into the night. The moon was full, so she could see where the road was. She wanted to run somewhere, but where? Where could she go now? She heard footfalls behind her, and she was roughly grabbed by the arm. "Let me go!"

Cat was yanked around to face Henderson. "Don't you ever do that again!" he growled. "Now come in and finish your dinner."

Feeling angry and betrayed, she let herself be pulled back to the house. Bill stood at the door with his mask in place, but she saw sadness in his eyes. They stopped at the door of the dining room. Before Henderson was able to say anything, Cat said quietly, "Father, take me home."

Henderson whirled around. "Sit and eat your dinner!"

"No," she replied. "Father, if you don't take me home, I'll walk."

Albert dabbed his mouth with the napkin. "I think this evening is over. Thank you for your hospitality, Logan." He rose, making a motion to John and Polly to do the same.

Cat could feel Henderson's anger radiating from him. "Albert, your daughter has to learn her place. Quit indulging her!"

Albert hesitated. "Cat, they went to a lot of trouble with this meal. We should at least be grateful for the food."

Cat wrestled internally, wanting to please her father but wanting to get away from Henderson. With a rasp, she said, "I'm sorry, Father, but I can't."

Henderson grabbed her shoulder and shook her. "That's enough out of you!"

Albert came to her defense and wrenched them apart. "No more, Logan. I won't have you hurting her in anger." John and Polly were behind him. He turned to them. "Let's go." Bill arrived with their things.

Henderson seethed. "You'll be sorry for this, Albert. You gave me your word."

Albert slipped on his gloves. "You know something? I'm beginning to regret everything. Goodnight, Logan. Thank you for your—hospitality."

Cat tied her cape and shuddered at the glare Henderson gave her father and her as they left the porch. Safely in the carriage and on the dark way back, she turned to him. "Henderson has something over you, doesn't he?"

"Don't worry about that now, Cat. Tomorrow is another day." He said no more the rest of the way home. Cat was beginning to feel uneasy about her father. Did Henderson control what Albert did? And why? When they reached the house, Polly gave her a quick hug before she and John turned to the path to their house. They said their goodnights and went in.

****

Jake was busy at his desk, trying to sort his stories for the newspaper before the deadline. Taking time to run back and forth to the Callahan ranch had cut into his work schedule, and Harvey was not pleased. He came over with a note paper in his hand and gave it to Jake. "I want a piece for Ed Matthews' wedding reception. He's getting married to Edna Harper at the courthouse, and the Grand is throwing them a reception at the dining hall. I want you to be at the hotel at seven in the evening, sharp, this Friday."

"But I—"

Harvey pursed his lips. "I don't care if you have plans already. You've been lollygagging around, not getting your work in. You're lucky I don't fire you." He turned on his heel and went back to his desk.

Jake suddenly had a headache. He *knew* Cat was going to be there. What if she came with Henderson? He couldn't have a scene like what happened at the restaurant, not at a wedding reception. He hastily wrote a note and sealed it in an envelope. *Maybe if I escort Peggy, Henderson will leave me alone.*

Sidling up to Jim, the courier, he gave it to him. "Can you get this to Miss Peggy Spencer by Thursday? She's at the Callahan ranch. And wait for a reply."

Jim nodded. "I've a message to drop off near there tomorrow, and I'll take yours, too."

Jake flipped him a quarter. "Thanks." He headed back to his desk to finish up his stories for the typesetter.

****

Cat set her jaw. "Father, why can't I take Sage into town? I've been riding her around the ranch, and you said I could have her. I need some things from the general store for Edna's wedding." She pulled on her riding gloves, picked up the saddlebags, and was stopped at the door by Albert.

"What's the matter with you, girl? You can't go gallivanting all over God's creation without an escort." He had his jaw set, as well.

She stomped her foot. "I came clear across country without one. Why can't I go into town?"

He glared. "Lord, child, you're defiant! See if Polly will go with you. Nell can watch the children."

"All right. I'll ask her." Deep down, Cat welcomed the company, but she wouldn't let her father see that. The late October morning was sunny, but a bit of a chill wind was blowing, and Cat shivered as she made her way to the cabin. The weather wasn't changeable as it was in Virginia, but she was told some of the winter rainstorms could be cold. The sweet, pungent smell of Polly's cooking fire met her nose.

She climbed the porch steps and rapped on the door frame. "Polly! May I see you?"

Polly appeared, wiping her hands on her apron. "Cat. What is it?"

"Could you go into town with me?" She explained about her dilemma.

Polly hesitated. "Well, I do need a few things in town. I'll get the buckboard. That will take a few minutes. Could you get the children up to the house?" Cat nodded. "Sam! Aggie! Go up with Auntie to the house."

The children piled out the door and jumped around Cat. "We heard you're going to town," Sam said. "What are you going to buy?"

Polly admonished him, "Now, that wasn't nice. Don't think you're always going to get something from the store."

The boy hung his head. "Sorry, Ma."

Cat took hold of both children's hands. "Come now. We'll be back in no time." Sam and Aggie smiled and skipped alongside her. Cat thought about changing out of her riding clothes but didn't want to take time for the bustles and petticoats. After depositing the two with the maid, Cat sat on the porch waiting for Polly, and in a few minutes the rattling of the wagon over the ruts and the clomping of the horses' hooves set her off down the steps.

Polly had taken off her apron and put on her

sunbonnet. Her work dress was clean, but she didn't have her bustle, either. She drew the buckboard in front of the house. "Ready?" she called.

Cat put her foot on the front wheel hub and swung up onto the wooden seat beside Polly. The springs squeaked as the wagon tipped back into position. "Thank you for doing this for me."

Polly waved her hand. "Don't think of it." She snapped the reins, and the two horses tripped lively down the drive.

Cat opened the parasol to shield her from the relentless Arizona sun. They talked about mundane things on the way. Cat marveled at how Polly came out of her shell once she knew someone.

At the general store, they stopped in front of the double doors and hopped out. They both gave their lists to the shopkeeper and looked at the new shipment of fabrics that had come in that week. Cat decided to get several yards of the new lace to freshen up her blue dinner dress for the reception and found a sprig of silk violets for the bodice.

They paid for their purchases and carried them out to the wagon. As Cat was hoisting herself onto the seat, a flapping white envelope caught her eye. It had been tacked on the side of the buckboard. "Wait a moment! There's something here."

Polly was already in the seat with the reins in her hands. "What is it?"

Cat pulled the tack out of the wooden side. "It's an envelope with my name on it." At a loss to know what it was doing there, she stuffed it into her reticule and climbed up next to Polly. "Let's go. I'll look at it on the way back."

On the part of the road going out of town that wasn't quite as rough, she pulled out the envelope and read the paper inside.

Miss Monroe, if you value your life, stay away from Logan Henderson. A friend.

A startled "Oh!" came from her mouth.

Polly glanced at her. "What is it?"

"I've gotten two warnings to stay away from Logan Henderson. One from his butler and now this." Cat waved the paper for emphasis. "Do you know why Father always goes along with Henderson?"

Polly shook her head. "I don't hear all the discussions between him, John, and Logan. I do know there's been some fiery arguments, but Logan seems to get his way."

Cat prayed he would just leave her alone. After she removed her purchases from the back of the buckboard, she waved as Polly drove back to the barn. Albert was leaving on his daily inspection of the cattle. She motioned him over. Shading her eyes, she said, "Father, could you be my escort to Edna's wedding Friday?"

He paused for a moment. "I would be honored." He inclined his head and rode off.

Chapter 13

Jake and Peggy took a seat at a far table in the Grand's spacious dining room. Festive ribbons of many colors bedecked the chandeliers, and small vases with fall flowers graced the tables arranged around a dance floor. The center carpets had been removed to accommodate dancing, and a small ensemble readied their instruments before the wedding party arrived. Jake busily jotted the descriptions in his notebook and glanced at Peggy, who was studying him carefully.

"Finally come up for air?" she asked with a hint of humor in her eyes. "You can't very well hide behind your notebook all evening."

Jake twisted his face. "If I could, I would have worn a suit made with the same print as the wallpaper. Harvey knew I was uneasy about coming here."

Townspeople drifted in, dressed in their finest, and took seats while waiting for the newly wedded couple to enter. Ed may not have any family here, but he was a respected member of the community, in his church, and as a member of the Odd Fellows.

To Jake's relief, a large family took seats at a table in front of them, and he was able to observe the festivities, watching between the members. One of the waiters strode to the stage, spoke to the ensemble, and in a moment the leader whispered to the others and they began to play the wedding march from *A Midsummer*

Night's Dream. As they played, the wedding party came in and took their places at the head table. Edna looked regal in a dark blue taffeta dress with white lace and a white hat with ostrich feathers. Ed was in a dark suit and a starched white shirtfront and collar. He kept tugging at the collar as he sat down.

Peggy poked Jake's arm with her fan. "There's Cat. She's not with Henderson."

Jake felt some ease to his anxiety as he saw Cat enter on the arm of her father. They sat at the head table as the best man and his wife did also. Cat was beautiful in her light blue dinner dress, and Jake felt his chest and groin tighten.

Peggy poked him again. "It's not polite to stare. Anyway, they're starting to serve the appetizers."

A couple of latecomers sat down next to Jake and Peggy, introducing themselves and starting a conversation Jake didn't particularly want to follow. The rotund, balding man was sweating profusely, saying he was a bartender at the Oriental, where Ed came in occasionally after work. An iced plate of oysters was placed in front of them, and the bartender ended up with the most, slurping noisily. Most of the meal was like that, with Jake amazed at the amount of food the man could pack into his mouth at one time.

The meal ended with the fruited bride's cake. Peggy wrapped her piece of it in her handkerchief, as was a maiden's tradition, and put it in her reticule. She would transfer it that night to a place under her pillow and would supposedly dream of her intended. Jake didn't believe in old wives' tales.

As the dishes were cleared, the ensemble changed from soft dinner music to waltzes and polkas. For the first waltz, the new Mr. and Mrs. Matthews glided onto the dance floor. After a few minutes, others followed, until the area was filled with happy people. Jake caught a glimpse of Cat and her father as they whirled by. Peggy swayed to the music.

She gave him a glare. "Well, are you going to ask me to dance, or are you going to fritter away with your notes all night?"

Jake scowled. "I didn't come here to dance. I'm here on assignment."

"Oh, fiddle-dee-dee!" She grabbed him by the arm and hauled him up.

They stepped out on the dance floor and fell into a lively polka. Jake tried to keep his head down, hoping Cat wouldn't catch a glimpse of him. This was not the time or place for a long explanation and apology. When the music stopped, he heard a commotion coming from the head table. Cat was hugging Edna, and Albert was shaking Ed's hand, and then the Monroes turned and— Cat ran into Jake. She appeared stricken again.

Jake involuntarily said, "Cat, wait."

She drew herself up. "It's Miss Monroe to you. Excuse me!" And she huffed out, followed by her father, who gave Jake the evil eye. John and Polly, who were at another table, rose and left, as well. Peggy appeared at his elbow.

"I'm sorry, Jake. I shouldn't have made you dance with me."

He sighed. "Never mind, Sis. She probably would have spotted me anyway. I'm curious why Henderson didn't escort her."

"Maybe you have more of a chance with her than you think. The masquerade ball is a week from tomorrow. You can approach Cat without her knowing who you are."

"I don't have a costume, let alone a mask."

She kissed his cheek. "Leave it to me, big brother. I'll make costumes for both of us."

Jake went to collect his things from the table, and he and Peggy congratulated Mr. and Mrs. Matthews. As they were saying their goodbyes, Edna took him aside.

In a hushed voice, she said, "That's your sister?" At Jake's nod, she added, "Cat thinks she's your new beloved."

Jake coughed. "So that's why she acted like she did." Of course she'd never met Peggy, so she didn't know. Apparently, her family didn't tell her, either.

Edna squeezed Jake's hand. "She doesn't want to see Henderson again. I'm sure you can win her back."

After thanking Edna and offering congratulations once more, Jake left with Peggy, feeling lighter than he had in weeks.

****

Cat climbed into the carriage and buried her face in her hands. Polly sat beside her and gently rested her fingers on Cat's arm. "What's wrong, Cat?"

Cat sniffed. "I didn't want to stay and see Jake with that woman."

"That woman? That's his sister, Peggy."

Albert cleared his throat over the last few words. Cat leaned in toward Polly. "Did you say, his sister?"

Albert growled. "Polly, mind your business!"

Cat glared at her father. "You knew that all the time and didn't tell me?"

"I don't want you seeing him again."

"Father, Jake was always a kind gentleman to me.

Logan Henderson wants to control me, and I fear what he would do to me if we wed."

He glared back. "Remember, he used you to get a story."

"I was too hasty in condemning him. He was on the story before we fell in love."

"Stuff and nonsense, girl. You don't know what love is. Love is finding someone who can support you for the rest of your life, like Henderson."

She shuddered. "There is something wrong with him. He has no pictures or mementos of his wife. And he changes the subject every time I ask about her. I fear he has no soul."

John spoke up. "Pa, it may not be my place, but I think Jake would be a better suitor for Cat."

Albert frowned. "You're right. It's not your place."

Cat went home with mixed feelings. She was relieved that Jake wasn't seeing another woman, but her father refused to listen to anything she had to say, and that distressed her.

The next morning, she opened her trunk and pulled out a package wrapped in brown paper. It was a costume she'd worn to a masquerade ball in Virginia shortly before she left. So much work had gone into it, she couldn't bear to leave it behind. Opening the package, she shook it out and spread it over her coverlet. She had gone as the fairy queen Titania from *A Midsummer Night's Dream*. The light brown and moss green netting was cut into many leaves for the skirt, and that was echoed on the long flowing sleeves that were gathered above the elbow. The bodice was green velvet, with silk flowers fastened around the scooped neckline. Small flowers and fall leaves bedecked the netting. A flower wreath for her hair, a green mask, and a pair of green velvet slippers completed the outfit.

Checking it over, she saw it had come through the long journey without much wear and tear. A few stitches should secure the netting again. She would borrow Polly's dress form and get to work for next Saturday.

The afternoon of the ball, Cat was seated at her vanity while Nell painstakingly took one of the two curling irons out of the fireplace and wound a long tress of Cat's hair around it. It sizzled some from the dampness, but at least it didn't burn. After an hour, ringlets flowed to her waist. Cat put on her slippers, and Nell helped her into her dress, lacing it tight in back.

"Miss Cat, you look like a storybook princess!" she gushed.

Cat twirled around. "Do you really think so?" She sat in front of the mirrored vanity again, and Nell pinned the wreath onto her curls. She slipped her mask with the thin ribbon ties into her reticule to be put on later.

"Cat, are you ready?" called her father from downstairs.

"In a moment!" Cat did a quick swipe with rouge on her cheeks and lips and hurried to the front hall. She was reaching for her hooded cape when her father came in, dressed in colonial clothes with a powdered wig and a tri-cornered hat.

"Catherine! I can see your ankles! That gown is indecent." He tugged her arm around so she faced him.

"This is a masquerade, Father. People dress in all sorts of outfits. I've even seen girls in ballerina skirts that are just below the knee." She threw her cape around her shoulders and drew the hood up. "Yes, I'm ready."

He huffed as he put his cape on and opened the door for her. John and Polly were already in the carriage, waiting. She climbed in and sat across from Polly.

The late October evening was starting to get frosty, and their breaths caught in the night air. Even in southern Arizona Territory the long nights were cold even if the days were still mild. Polly told her they could get a dusting of snow occasionally in the storms from the mountains. Steam rose from the horses as they trotted the road into town.

Cat anticipated seeing Jake again and hoped he would be there. *I would like for him to forgive my rudeness, and I can forgive him for putting my story in the newspaper.*

The hall was brightly lit and cast a warm glow through the windows and doors. They could hear the orchestra sending streamers of music out into the night air. When Albert had guided the horses to the main entrance, John helped Cat and Polly down.

Albert called out, "Escort the girls in, and I'll take care of the carriage."

John, in a pioneer jacket and breeches, both with leather fringe, showed the tickets at the door and took the girls' capes. Polly was in a sleeveless thin leather Indian squaw dress that had fringe from her knees to the floor. Beading in beautiful patterns played across the front, and she wore a silver-and-turquoise necklace. Her hair, in long braids, was adorned with a beaded headband.

Both girls gushed, "What a lovely costume!" at the same time and then laughed together.

When John came back, he and the two girls tied on their masks and went into the ballroom.

The room seemed to roil from the couples dancing and everyone swaying to the waltz music. Cat scanned the crowd, but it was hard to tell who was who with the costumes and masks. Gaily-colored streamers and rubber balloons hung from the chandeliers, and garish bunting trimmed the walls.

John turned to them. "Let's go to that empty table over there and wait for Pa."

They sat down, and Cat saw a pirate dressed in black except for a white shirt with classic large sleeves gathered at the wrist. He seemed familiar, though he wore a patch over one eye. He swept off his hat with the large ostrich feather and bowed low in front of her.

"Wouldst fair lady desire a dance with me?"

Cat laughed. "Yes, I would love to." She winked at Polly as she sailed onto the floor.

He smiled. "May I introduce myself?"

With a teasing poke, she said, "You don't have to." His expression was wicked.

At the end of the number, Jake squeezed her hand. "Let's go where we can talk."

Cat noticed her father had joined the others. "We could go outside for a moment," she said. They slipped out the door on the other side of the ballroom and into a small vestibule.

Jake removed his hat and looked contrite. "I'm sorry I didn't tell you about the story I was working on. I should have done so when my feelings for you changed."

She sighed. "I guess I was really hurt by that, but I do accept your apology. I owe you one, as well." His forehead puckered. "I thought you had taken up with someone else."

"What made you think that?"

"I saw you with another girl twice. But then I found out it was your sister."

He laughed. "So that was why you were so angry with me. That was Peggy. She got back a couple of weeks ago from San Francisco. I'm here with her tonight." His face grew tender. "I really missed you, Cat." His arms went around her, and as he kissed her Cat marveled at the heat they generated in their thin costumes. Her chest and belly tightened. She could hardly catch her breath.

He pushed back and took a long look at her. "You look like a picture-book princess tonight."

The corners of her mouth curled up. "I'm dressed like Titania, the fairy queen."

A teasing sparkle set in his eyes. "I should have dressed to match you."

"You mean, come as Oberon, the king?"

"No. As Bottom, with the head of an ass."

They embraced again. "You do look very dashing as a pirate." She moved her hand into his. "Come. I should like to meet your sister."

They reentered the ball room, and Jake nodded toward a couple on the dance floor. "Peggy is the female harlequin over there." They waited until the music stopped and the dancers were coming to the tables while the orchestra had a break. Jake made the introductions, and while Cat was getting to know Peggy, she felt someone grab her by her loose hair and yank her back, accompanied by, "I told you to stay away from her!"

Cat gasped and was nearly pulled over, but she regained her footing and was able to turn enough to see that a man in an early 1800s suit and top hat was holding onto her. "Take your hands off me!"

Jake stood in front of him. "Miss Monroe wants no part of you, Henderson!"

"I told you this wasn't finished, Spencer!" And he tried to land a fist on Jake's jaw, an attempt which was deflected. Jake grabbed him by the shoulders and threw him to the floor. Henderson tripped Jake, and they rolled over, trading blows.

As the crowd gathered to watch the two combatants, Sheriff Cortland and one of his deputies pulled them apart. "What is going on here?"

Henderson pointed at Jake. "He was interfering with my intended."

Cat, who was watching with horror from the sidelines, belted out, "I'm not your intended!"

The sheriff thought for a moment. "Mr. Henderson, since you are who you are, I'm going to let you two sort this out peacefully. If you can't do it peacefully, I'm putting you both in jail."

By that time, Albert and John had joined them. Henderson turned to Albert and pointed at Cat. "I wish you would control your daughter."

Cat felt her whole body tense with a desire to get a gun and blow Henderson to kingdom come. "I can't take this any more!" she exploded. "Father, I told you how I feel. If you insist on Mr. Henderson courting me, I will have to move out."

"Cat, listen—" Albert moved to put a hand on her

shoulder, but she shook him off.

"Leave me alone! Why can't everybody leave me alone!" She ran out the side door and into the carriage lot, where she untied her mask, leaned on one of the hitching posts, and burst into tears full of hurt, anger, and frustration. She heard someone come over to her.

"May I help?"

She turned, and Polly was there. "What's going on in there?"

Polly embraced her. "The three are glaring at each other in a Mexican standoff. I'm guessing if one went after you the others would fight him."

Cat pulled back and raised her hands in a pleading gesture. "What am I going to do? Everyone thinks they know better than I do what's for my own good. Why do men *do* that?" Polly just shook her head. Cat took a handkerchief out of her reticule and dried her face.

In another few minutes, Albert came up, with John behind him, and they were carrying the girls' capes. "Put these on. We're going home."

Cat was tying her hood when they heard two shots go off, just around the corner of the building from where they stood. Everyone ran toward the sound, and then Cat screamed. Jake was down, clutching his arm where the red of blood was soaking it, and Henderson was in a heap on the other side of the walk. She heard horse hoofs beating down the dark street and caught a glimpse of a figure riding away. The white tail of the fleeing horse waved like a beacon. She ran to Jake and dropped down beside him. Peggy struggled through the crowd and exclaimed, "Oh, no! Jake!" She knelt on the other side of him.

Albert went to Henderson and rolled him over.

"Where is Doc Riley?" Albert called to the crowd. A short balding man dressed in a fanciful soldier's uniform squeezed out between the stunned people.

The doc checked Henderson for breathing and a heartbeat and found neither. "He's dead, Albert," he said finally.

The sheriff, who was watching the proceedings, looked around the body before he stalked to Jake and hauled him up. Jake moaned in pain. "You're under arrest for murder, Spencer. Henderson was unarmed." He picked up Jake's gun.

"I...didn't shoot him, Sheriff. If you look...that gun hasn't...been fired." The doc caught Jake as he passed out, lowering him to the ground. Cat cradled his head as Peggy rubbed his hand until he came to again.

Meanwhile, the sheriff examined the weapon. "The barrel is cold, and there are six rounds in the chambers." He glanced at Jake. "Tell me what happened."

Doc came back with his bag and was tending to Jake's arm. Jake took a shaky breath. "After Albert and John went to get their things, Henderson told me to meet him outside. I didn't trust him, so I stopped to strap on my gun. Henderson stood across the walkway from the entrance." He paused as if trying to build up his strength. "I came out and heard Henderson say, 'Here, Spencer,' and then two shots came from the corner of the building. One hit Henderson and one hit me."

Cat spoke up. "When I came around to see what had happened, I saw someone riding away in that direction." She pointed to the north of town.

The sheriff studied her. "Did you see who it was?"

"No, sir. It was too dark."

Doc nodded. "The direction would be right. Henderson was hit in the back." He helped Jake up. "Come with me, boy. I have to get that bullet out."

Cat rose and squeezed his hand. "I'll go with you."

Jake kissed her on the forehead. "No. You go home and get some rest. I'll be all right."

Peggy put her hand on Cat's shoulder. "I'll let you know what happens."

Cat glanced at Albert. "You'll let her come over?" He hesitated, then gave a curt nod. She turned back to Peggy. "Please stop by." Cat gave Jake's hand a final squeeze before she followed her family to the carriage.

****

The bullet made a small ping when Doc dropped it from the medical tweezers to the little basin. Jake felt like a saber had been pushed through his arm muscles.

Doc poured some liquid from a dark medicine bottle into a shot glass. "Here. Drink this. Then I want you to lie down in my back room bed tonight."

Jake sniffed at the contents. "What is it?"

"Laudanum. It will kill the pain and help you sleep." Doc finished closing the wound and wrapped it.

Peggy rose from a chair and stood beside Jake. "Will he be all right?"

Doc nodded. "I just want to keep an eye on him for a day, to make sure there's no infection."

Peggy and the doctor got on either side of Jake and helped him to bed. Peggy lightly put her hand on his cheek. "I'll be back tomorrow with Cat."

Jake felt like he was underwater and going down fast. All he could do was smile. As doc removed his boots, he drifted off into darkness.

Chapter 14

Cat finished saddling Sage, one of her father's mares. The gentle brown-and-gray horse happily munched on a bit of carrot Cat had brought. Last night she'd heard loud voices coming from outside, but she couldn't hear the words they were saying. She kept thinking about that, but right now Peggy waited for her out in the yard, on Mazie. With a scratch of Sage's nose, Cat led her out of the stable and mounted up.

Cat had been shocked that Peggy chose to wear denims and a flannel shirt, but she explained to Cat that working with her father and Mr. Callahan, it was much easier than with all the flounces. Cat felt overdressed in her riding clothes and veiled, broad-brimmed hat. Ladies would never think of wearing men's clothes in Virginia. She'd have to get over her upbringing now that she was out west.

The girls set off on the road to town. Cat glanced at Peggy. "How was Jake when you left him?"

Peggy told Cat everything that had happened in the doctor's office. "Doc is very good and used to patching up gunshot wounds. I'm not worried." She paused. "What I am worried about is *why* he and Henderson were shot."

Cat pondered that, like she had most of her sleepless night. "I wish I could have had a better look at who was riding away. I suspect that was the one who shot them."

When they rode into town, Peggy led the way to Doc's office. They dismounted and tied the horses by the communal trough and let them drink. Peggy lifted a brown paper package from her saddlebags. "I brought some of pa's clothes to have Jake change into." She chuckled. "We can't have him wandering through town dressed like a pirate."

Doc was at his desk when the girls came in. He looked up. "Morning, Miss Spencer, Miss Monroe."

Peggy handed him the package. "I've brought clothes for Jake to change into."

He took the package and waved toward a couple of chairs. "I'll take it back to him. Have a seat."

When he returned, he sat down and faced them. "Jake can leave this morning, but I want him to rest for a few days." He turned to Peggy. "Can you stay with him tonight?" She nodded.

Cat was going through inner turmoil with worry for Jake. She couldn't quite put her finger on what was bothering her, but it loomed like a storm cloud on the horizon. Then she realized it was what Peggy had said. *Why were he and Henderson shot? Is Jake still in danger?*

Doc poured some liquid from a medicine bottle into an empty one and corked it. "Miss Spencer, I want you to give him a teaspoonful of this painkiller before bed tonight, but then only if he really needs it tomorrow. And change the dressing. I want him to come back in two days." He wrapped some gauze and tape in a small piece of brown paper and tied a string around it.

The door to the back room opened, and Jake leaned against the frame, grinning. "You two are a sight for sore eyes." He was pale but put on a good face. He had the pirate costume tucked in the brown paper under his arm.

Cat and Peggy went to him in an instant. Cat said, "Do you think you can ride?" She glanced questioningly at Doc.

"If he takes it easy getting on, he should be all right," Doc replied.

Cat and Peggy took stations on either side of Jake and helped him down the stairs to the waiting horses. Peggy thought for a moment. "Jake, you ride Mazie, and I'll walk the sidewalk to your apartment." She took the package from him.

"Whatever you say, Sis." With help from both of them, he was able to climb onto the patient horse.

Cat mounted Sage and rode beside him to the apartment, while Peggy kept up with them on the walk. "Jake, I noticed you didn't tell the sheriff last night if you saw who shot you."

He shook his head. "I didn't get a good look at him. Just saw a dark figure jump on a horse as soon as the shots were fired."

They rounded the corner, and Peggy stood in front of a building that Cat assumed was where Jake's apartment was located. They helped him up the steps and into his room. Cat was amazed at the sparse furnishings and bare walls, a typical bachelor accommodation.

Peggy pulled the curtains back and opened the windows to let the cool morning air move in and freshen the stale smell of a closed room. The Saturday market noise from the street clattered and stomped in, as well. Peggy tsked as she went through his cupboard.

"You don't have anything but coffee here."

Jake sat on the bed with his feet up. "I don't eat here."

Cat stood by Peggy. "Why don't you brew some coffee, and I'll go down the street to the bakery?" She checked her reticule for coins and went downstairs to the street, where she carefully picked her way across the road through the garbage and animal waste to the walk that went to the little shops a block away. She felt better now that she knew Jake was going to be all right; she also felt a certain amount of guilt for her relief that Henderson was dead.

The aroma of warm bread that met her as she reached the bakery window made her stomach growl, and she did not delay going inside. The bell on the door tinkled merrily. A round, jovial man greeted her at the counter. "Morning, miss. What would you like?"

She inspected the baked goods on the shelves behind the glass. "I'd like a loaf of bread, please, and three of those crullers. Are they all fresh?"

"Yes, miss. Made this morning." He wrapped the goods in brown paper, and she counted out the coins for payment. Her next stop was at the grocery next door, where the proprietor kept fresh sausages and cheese on ice. She bought a pound of sliced salami and a pound of cheddar.

As she was walking out of the shop, she noticed Ned Hadley riding past Jake's apartment. *Don't tell me Father sent his foreman to spy on me.* Ned stopped by Sage and looked up at the windows. She picked her way back across the street. "Anything you want, Mr. Hadley?"

His head whipped around like a lazy susan. "What

are you doing here?"

"It really isn't any of your concern. What are *you* doing here?"

"Passing through. Had some business in town and noticed Sage hitched here."

She paused, wanting to hit his horse on the rump to make him leave. "Tell Father I'll be home in a few hours. You may go."

He turned his horse around. "You're danged lucky you're a woman." He spit on the ground and rode off.

She went upstairs to Jake's apartment. Jake had a steaming cup sitting on his nightstand. Peggy was pouring two more mugs of coffee and took Cat's parcels from her.

"I'll slice the bread and make the sandwiches. Go sit down."

Cat set one of the wooden chairs next to Jake's bed and set her mug on the stand. "How are you feeling?"

He gave her a grimace. "Harvey stopped by from the paper to see me. He gave me the lecture again that I was to report news, not be it. I guess I still have a job. He didn't say 'fired' at all."

"It wasn't your fault Henderson was such a hothead. Although I shouldn't think ill of the dead." *Even as I want to leap for joy.*

Peggy set another chair beside Cat's, then handed them each a sandwich and a cruller. They talked as they ate, and Cat learned stories of their ranch life growing up. A couple of hours flew by, and Cat found herself very content in their company, as if she had known them all her life.

As Peggy stored the leftover food in the cupboard, Cat sat on the edge of Jake's bed. They both looked at

Peggy, who suddenly went to the door. "I think I'll unsaddle Mazie and take her to the stable."

Cat put her hand on Jake's cheek. "I wish I didn't have to go, but Father will be on tenterhooks if I linger any longer."

He put his fingers over hers, and his lips brushed her palm. Her whole body tingled. "I didn't like being without you. I love you, Cat." They shared a sweet farewell kiss.

Cat reluctantly rose and got her things together. At the door, she paused. "I love you, too, Jake." Her heart swelled as his intense gaze burned into her soul. She closed the door and hurried down the stairs.

Peggy came across the road while Cat was unhitching Sage. "Be careful going home."

Cat mounted Sage. "I won't go out of my way to attract attention. Take good care of Jake for me."

Peggy waved. "You bet!"

As Cat turned onto the main street, she heard, "Cat! Wait up!"

She looked around as her brother Daniel rode up beside her. "Where are you going all by yourself?"

"I was here to see Jake, and now I'm going home."

He nodded. "I heard what happened at the ball last night. How is he?"

She told him what had been going on. "I thought you'd be working in the mine today."

"The price of silver has gone down on the market, so they're slowing production. I got an extra day off." He paused. "You shouldn't be going home by yourself. I'll escort you."

She opened her mouth to protest, but the thought of having company pleased her, so she shut it again. "All right."

A scuffle between two men was taking place in front of the Oriental Saloon, and they slowed their horses down. The larger of the two bashed his fist into the other's face, and the recipient went down in the street like a log. The large man turned, and Cat gasped. It was Whiskey Jones.

Jones caught sight of Daniel. "Monroe!" He weaved as he moved toward them. "I vowed to shoot ya next time I saw ya."

Cat moved her nervous horse between Jones and her brother. "Let him go by, you drunken sot!"

"You gol dang little hussy!" He lunged for her horse.

"Cat! Look out!" Daniel yelled.

She wheeled Sage around and saw that Jones had gone for his gun. Sage took off to the other side of the road, and while Cat's back was turned she heard two shots. Her heart felt like it would burst, and she was afraid to look behind her. The sheriff ran out of his office, so she turned as he passed.

Jones lay moaning in the street, and Daniel was still on his horse. A large crowd watched the proceedings. The sheriff barked at Daniel, "What happened here?"

Daniel related what had taken place. "I pulled my gun when he did. Luckily, I was sober."

The sheriff looked at the crowd. "Is he telling the truth?"

The ones who had witnessed the incident confirmed his story. One of the deputies came running up. "Should I get him to Doc's?"

The sheriff nodded. "Stay on guard there, and then

escort him to jail when Doc's done patching him up."
He turned to Daniel. "You may go, Monroe."

Daniel joined Cat, and they started back through
the crowd. "You see why you need an escort?" He
paused a moment. "Thanks for getting between us. That
was a brave thing you did."

She smirked. "That about scared me to pieces, but I
couldn't think of anything else to do."

They rode out of town without any further incident.
A light conversation drifted between them on the way
to the ranch. Daniel wanted to know about Virginia,
because he was so young when he left. Cat filled him in
on the area after the war. Soon they were at the gate for
Sugar Springs.

Cat waved a hand at the ranch. "Why don't you
come in for a while?"

He shook his head. "Pa still isn't taking kindly to
me. I'd rather not." He tipped his hat. "I'll see you
around town, Sis." He turned his horse and started back.

She rode down the drive and found her father on
the porch when she got to the house. He took out his
pocket watch and glanced at it. "Cat, I'll unsaddle Sage.
Do you have a mourning gown?"

"Yes, I do. Why?"

"We're going to the Henderson ranch for his burial
in two hours."

"But—"

"No back talk from you, girl. He was our neighbor,
and we have to have respect for the dead."

Arguing would get her nowhere. "Yes, Father. I'll
get Nell to help me change clothes." Deep down, she
wanted to dance on Henderson's grave.

Two hours later, Cat climbed into the carriage, with

John and Polly across from her. She picked at her black crepe sleeve. Albert hopped into the driver's seat and snapped the whip. The horses set off at a fast clip-clop.

There were a number of carriages in the yard as they drove up. Reverend Phillips from St. Paul's was greeting everyone as they went up the steps into the fine home. He grasped Cat's hand as she walked up to the door. "I'm so, so sorry, my dear, for your loss."

She hesitated. "My loss?"

He nodded. "Of your intended. He and your father visited me only last week to plan your wedding."

Her breath went out of her. She must have stared stupidly at him, because her father swept her away. "She's grief stricken right now. Please excuse us, Reverend." He hauled her into the alcove next to the stairs.

"Wedding?" she barked. "You went to plan my wedding?"

"Shh, keep your voice down."

"How dare you, Father! I told you I never wanted to have anything to do with that man!" She wanted to hit, kick, or spit on something, but she held her temper.

Albert's mouth pressed in a tight line. "We'll talk about this at home. Don't embarrass me in front of the neighbors."

She huffed. "I'll behave, but don't expect me to wear widow's weeds for the next few years. I did not agree to marry him." This was worse than what Jake had done to her. Why did everyone take her for granted without asking what she thought? Her father offered his arm. She hesitated, but at his glare, put her hand through it.

John and Polly sat in the back row in the parlor on

the folding wooden seats the undertaker provided. Her father tried to lead her to the front, but she held her feet firm until he shrugged and moved to the two empty seats next to his son and daughter-in-law.

Cat didn't listen to the service until she heard her name mentioned as the bereaved intended. Everyone glanced around at her, and she was seething again. Albert and John were two of the pallbearers, and after the parlor had emptied of people, Cat and Polly stood outside in the back of the crowd and waited for the casket to be taken to the small fence-enclosed family plot where Mrs. Henderson had been buried.

The reverend recited the burial service, then made a motion toward Cat to come over. He handed her the gravedigger's shovel, and she understood that she was supposed to throw in the first dirt on the coffin. That she did gleefully. Somehow, though, she managed some decorum.

Many of the neighbors didn't go to her to express their condolences, out of either confusion or perhaps embarrassment. Most had gone to the masquerade and had seen her with Jake. *Oh, why did Father put me in this position? I have to live with these people now.*

Everyone went back inside the house for refreshments after the end of the burial service. Cat spotted Bill standing invisibly near the butler's pantry door. She waited until the neighbors had gathered into the parlor before going over to Bill.

"Bill?"

"Yes, Miss Monroe?"

"Why did you warn me to leave Tombstone and never come back, the last time I was here?"

Bill hesitated. "Because of what happened to Mrs.

Henderson."

"Tell me, Bill. I won't tell anyone else."

He turned to the butler's pantry and opened a drawer. He pulled out a small tin with Chinese symbols and a dragon on it. "Last week Mr. Henderson brought home this tin he bought from a Chinaman. It was the same tea he had given the missus when she kept getting sicker and sicker. I wanted to warn you somehow." He looked down with guilt. "I didn't want to betray Mr. Henderson. His family owned me and taught me how to behave and speak well. I stayed with Mr. Henderson as his butler after the war."

"Do you know where he got that?"

"In the Chinese part of Tombstone. I don't know exactly where."

"May I have that, Bill? I'd like to know what's in it."

He handed it to her. "Certainly, Miss Monroe."

She put it in her reticule just as her father came out of the parlor. "Catherine, where are your manners?"

"I'll be right there." She mouthed, "Thank you," to Bill as she turned to go. He gave her a slight bow.

She found Polly in the back of the parlor and joined her. "Where did you go, Cat?" she whispered.

"I don't want to discuss it here, but I got some information from the butler."

"On what?"

"Henderson." Cat shushed her and got a glass of punch. Callahan and the Spencers were there, but they didn't cause any scenes with the Monroes, merely ignored them. After an hour or so of socializing, people started drifting toward their carriages and leaving.

Albert expressed his thanks to the reverend, then

herded them to the carriage as the sun was starting to turn red on the horizon. Halfway home he said to Cat, "What were you talking to that darky about?"

Cat paused, not knowing what to tell him. "I was expressing thanks for all he had done for the guests." She hoped he would question no further.

Albert snorted. "That's his job. Pay him no mind, girl."

Polly opened her mouth to say something, but Cat shook her head no. They arrived at the house in the dim twilight and said their goodnights. Cat wheeled on her father after he closed the door.

"You humiliated me, Father! Why on God's green earth would you go behind my back and plan a wedding to a man I didn't want to marry?"

He slammed his hat down on the hall table. "It's a father's duty to fix up his daughter with someone who has the means to take care of her."

"I told you he was a cruel man. He wouldn't take care of me. He had no heart or soul in him. Fortunately, someone shot him before he got his hands on me."

His eyes snapped fire. "You and Daniel must have been cut from the same mold. You're both ungrateful and insolent."

"We must take after you. Goodnight, Father!" She turned on her heel and ran upstairs, slamming the bedroom door behind her. She rummaged for the lucifers, lit her desk lamp, and proceeded to unbutton her gown. Sitting down on the edge of her bed, she began to cry from frustration. *I wouldn't have made that quest to find Father if I'd known he was so stubborn.* She jumped at a knock on her door. "Who is it?"

"It's Nell, Miss Monroe. I've brought you some tea

and sandwiches."

She dried her face and opened the door. "Thank you, Nell." She took the tray and set it on her bedstand as Nell left, poured some tea into her cup, then remembered the tin in her reticule. Taking it out, she looked it over. On the bottom of the tin was pasted a label: Lee Tang, Purveyor of Fine Herbal Teas, Tombstone, with some Chinese characters. *I wonder if I could find out what's in this. But I don't remember a Lee Tang shop on Allen Street. Maybe Jake would know.* She resolved to go into town Monday and find out.

Chapter 15

Jake woke to the sound of Peggy coming in with her arms full of baked goods. "Morning, big brother. How are you feeling today?"

He stretched his stiff shoulder. "Still sore, but I was thinking about going to the office tomorrow. Got a lot of work to catch up on. Where did you get the bread and treats?"

Peggy started the pot of water on the heating stove for the coffee. "They had a fundraiser at church after service. I'll have breakfast with you, and then I'll go home, if you're sure you'll be all right."

Jake nodded. "Sure. Hear anything from Cat?"

She paused. "Just some dirt going around about Henderson's burial yesterday. I went to the morning service at St. Paul's, and tongues are wagging. The Monroes didn't show up this morning." She related what she'd heard. "Everyone was saying that for a bereaved intended she was acting as cold as a sleet storm."

"Why did everyone think she was his intended? An engagement was never announced."

"Because Henderson and Albert had been talking to the reverend about a wedding." Peggy pulled the pot of boiling water off the stove and added the coffee grounds.

"Poor Cat. Why would Albert want to do that to his

135

daughter?"

Peggy shook her head. "I don't know, but it's hurt her reputation. I do like Cat. Maybe we can help her some way."

Jake pondered that very thing while Peggy poured the coffee and put fresh homemade doughnuts on a plate. They bounced around a few ideas, not very good ones to Jake's way of thinking. Peggy left after she had cleaned the apartment, and Jake decided to go out for a walk and see what he could find out. Maybe Dara had heard something. It was getting toward noon, so she was probably up.

Dara's window was open, and when he took some pebbles and tossed them through, she stuck her head out of it, looking disheveled, still wearing her robe. She waved at him. "Give me a few minutes and I'll be down."

He kicked a few rocks until she came out the back door in a simple skirt and blouse, her hair tied at her nape. She made over his arm in the sling. "Hope it's getting better. I heard about the ball."

"Is there somewhere private we can go and talk? Most of the town is shuttered on Sunday."

She thought a moment. "We could go into the stable. Usually no one travels anywhere on a Sunday."

They climbed through the smaller opening in the big double door. The stable was warm in the cool morning air, and the rich equine smell hit his nostrils. She led him into the storage room, and they sat on a couple of crates.

He leaned toward her to ask, "Have you heard anything about the killing of Henderson?"

She shook her head. "Just speculation." She bit her

lip. "Can I confide in you?"

"What is it?"

"You're a reporter. You know how to search out things. Could you try to find out if Henderson killed his wife?"

Jake was silent for a moment. "What's that to you?"

She sighed. "I'm not who you think I am. I'm not Dara Foxwood, and I'm not from Tucson. My name is Ruby Buckley, and I'm from Texas."

Jake digested this information. "Buckley? Are you related to Henderson's wife?"

She nodded. "I'm her younger sister. I moved here after she died because I didn't believe Henderson's story. My sister was in good health when she married him, and then in only two years she sickened and died."

"Weren't you afraid he'd find you out?"

"I knew Henderson wouldn't go to a cat house, so I went to work here to keep an ear out and try to find some proof. Now I may never know for sure." She put her face in her hands. "I guess I should have moved quicker."

Something crossed Jake's mind. "You didn't shoot him, did you?"

"No. Anyway, I wouldn't have shot you, too." She pressed her lips together. "Why do you think I would?"

He put his hands up in surrender. "I'm sorry! I guess I'd like to know who's out gunning for me."

"I tried to warn Cat to get away from here. I didn't want to see anything happen to anyone else, like happened to Hallie."

"I don't remember Cat saying anything about that. When did you warn her?"

"She and Polly Monroe were at the general store, and I left an anonymous note tacked on their wagon. Would you please see what you can find out? Anything would help."

He nodded. "You've been a great help to me with information. Now it's my turn. I'll see what I can do."

Jake decided to do some sleuthing after going to the office first thing Monday morning.

****

Cat ran up the stairs to Jake's apartment and rapped on the door. There was no sound from inside, so she slowly opened it. The empty room was quiet and dark. *I wonder where he is? Could he have gone to the newspaper office?* She hurried down and mounted Sage. It was a short trip around the block to the *Epitaph*. She practically ran into Jake as he came out of the office. Both said, "What are you doing here?" at the same time.

Cat swallowed. Jake looked so handsome and welcoming, she wanted to melt in his arms right there. Her chest was tight, and her body was doing those strange things again.

"Cat?" His face held a spark of amusement.

"I—um, I brought something we need to check here in town."

He motioned to a bench in front of the newspaper office. "We can sit here. What is it?"

She pulled the tea out of her reticule and told him about Bill's warning and what he had said about the tea and Hallie Henderson. "I was wondering if you knew where this Chinese shop is, because I want to know what's in the tin."

He scratched his chin. "Lee Tang? That must be in

the Chinaman section of town. Not a good place for a lady."

"Go with me? I want to know if he was trying to poison me and if that was what happened to his first wife."

He thought for a moment. "Their main street is only a few blocks away. You can leave your horse here, and we can walk."

Even though his arm was still in a sling, he wore his gun. She felt safe with him. Cat put her hand on his good arm, and they started their trek. The Chinese section was seedy, and strange smells came from open windows of buildings. Some of what she smelled, she suspected, was from opium pipes. She had heard that many Chinese smoked opium, though she knew little about it other than it was a practice to be avoided. The people they passed watched them suspiciously.

Jake pointed at a sign painted on a shingle. There were Chinese characters and underneath it the English words Lee Tang, Proprietor. "That must be it."

A bell on the door announced their arrival, and a wizened little man greeted them in the shop. Cat thought he looked like paintings she had seen of Confucius, in his plain blue Chinese robe. He bowed and in fairly good English said, "May I help?"

Jake handed him the tin. "Can you tell us what is in this?"

Mr. Tang opened the tin and sniffed the contents. "Yes. Sold very short time ago. It *tong-huei*."

"Could it be poisonous to someone?"

"No, sir. Make loose bowels maybe, but not poison."

Cat bit her lip. "Do you remember who bought

139

this?"

Mr. Tang nodded. "Very well remember. Mr. Hennerson. He good customer when I sell to him in Tucson many year ago. He back last week. Want to buy same tea. Say he be married again."

Jake eyed him. "What does the tea do?"

"Very good for woman complaint. Blood flow good. Make better unease and pain. I prove not poison." He took the tin and poured some hot water into a teapot. Taking some of the tea out of the tin, Mr. Tang dropped it into the pot. In a few minutes, he poured the liquid into a cup. "Here. I drink." He took a swig of the tea and waited a moment. "Good *tong-huei*, not poison."

Jake retrieved the tin and gave it to Cat. "Thank you, Mr. Tang." Mr. Tang bowed as they went out the door. "Looks like Bill was wrong about this."

Cat stowed it in her reticule. "Unless something was wrong with Hallie's digestion and she couldn't tolerate the tea."

Jake shook his head. "She probably wouldn't continue to drink it if it bothered her."

Cat pursed her lips. "Maybe he forced her."

Jake was deep in thought as they walked back to the newspaper office. "Cat, I'd like you to meet a friend of mine. I think the two of you would be helpful to each other. But she has a job that you would not approve of."

"What's that?"

"A lady of the evening. She works at the Bird Cage."

Cat halted and looked him in the eye with a mixture of horror and suspicion. "Do you—?"

"No, I don't. But loose-lipped men do, and I get information secondhand, tips for stories I'm working on. I've gotten a lot of information from what she's heard." He hesitated. "She told me something that might interest you, but I want to find out if it's all right with her for you to know."

Cat had never associated with persons of that ilk, but she needed as much information as she could muster. Her father had to know what he had nearly gotten her into. She sighed. "All right. I'll talk to her. But do I have to go into that establishment?"

He took her by the hand. "No, of course not. I don't either, usually." He led her around back and picked up some pebbles and threw them at an upstairs window. They made a clattering sound, and then the sash went up. A female figure appeared. He waved. "Dara, can you come down?"

The figure waved back. "In a moment." The sash went back down.

In no time, a woman in a simple skirt and blouse came out the back door, and Cat realized it was the woman she had seen at the newspaper office. Jake indicated Cat. "Dara, this is Cat Monroe."

The woman smiled. "Yes, I know." She gave a slight bow. "I'm Dara Foxwood. Pleased to meet you."

Cat gave a faint grin. "Likewise."

Jake turned to Dara. "We've been on a quest today that you may be interested in, but I had to ask you first if you wanted to give Cat your information."

Dara hesitated. "I guess it would be all right, if you promise me, Cat, you won't tell anyone else."

Cat nodded. "I won't tell a soul."

Dara chewed on her lip. "I'm really Hallie Henderson's sister Ruby."

Cat gasped. "But why are you working as—"

"I was trying to find out anything I could on why my sister died. I wasn't home much anyway, wanted to be on my own, and the best money I could make was in the mining camps, so I became a fallen woman. I still care about my family, but they don't know what I do for a living." She went on to tell Cat what she had told Jake.

In return, Cat and Jake gave her the information they had gathered from their visit to the Chinese district of town.

Dara absorbed what was said. "Bill always seemed like a decent sort, but he was taught from early on to do what he was told. He must have been very worried, to give you that."

Cat agreed. "The fact that you gave me the same warning, anonymously, as he did made me want to find out if Henderson really wanted to kill me."

Dara was silent for a moment as a group of men walked by them. "Let me know anything you find out."

"I will." With that, Cat and Jake walked back to the street as Dara headed to the door of the building.

Jake offered his arm. "Let's have some lunch before you go to the ranch. Besides, I owe you for the food you brought the other day."

Cat put her arm through his. "Gladly." They went to a small restaurant on Allen Street and sat at a table by the window. As they chatted while they waited for their order, Cat glanced out the window and gasped. "Ned Hadley is on a bench across the street, looking at this building."

Jake looked too, then admonished her, "Don't stare outside. Make him think we didn't see him."

Anger boiled in her. "Father must have made him

come to spy on me."

Their order came, but the lightness of earlier gave way to suspicion. When they were finished, Jake paid for the lunch, and Cat hurried out just as Ned stood up. She shouted across the street, "Ned! What are you doing here?"

He looked like he was going to bolt, but he turned around. "Came into town for the mail."

She put both her fists on her hips, then pointed down the road. "The post office is that way, or are you lost?"

"Damn it, missy, you're bullheaded!"

"Don't use your foul language with me! I'll complain to my father!"

He spit on the ground. "You just do that, missy!" Then he turned on his heel and stomped away as Jake came out to join her.

"Well, he doesn't seem the worse for wear from that encounter." He chuckled.

Cat huffed. "That wasn't so amusing to me."

"Simmer down. Your father called the bloodhound out because you went into town by yourself, I would guess."

"I'd better go home before he calls out the army." They walked back to where Sage was waiting patiently. Cat placed her hand on the reins, but didn't unwind them from the hitching post.

Jake stood in front of her. "Something wrong?"

She gazed deep into his eyes. "I really want to stay with you." Love swelled in her chest, and she wanted to cry.

He ground his jaw, and his look bored into her. "Oh, Cat," he said, low. Then he took his hat off, put his

Ilona Fridl

good arm around her, and kissed her thoroughly. Beautiful warmth spread over her. A couple of whoops and catcalls made them jump apart.

Cat's cheeks burned, and she freed the reins. "I'm sorry. I'd better go."

Jake grinned solidly at her. "That'll give the gossips something else to natter about." He put his hat back on and helped her into the saddle.

She turned Sage around and blew him a kiss before riding down the street toward home. Leaving the outskirts, she heard hoofbeats a ways behind her. She pulled up Sage and looked around. "You might as well ride with me back to the ranch instead of sneaking in behind, Ned. I knew it was you."

"I reckon not. Prefer my own company."

She shrugged. "Suit yourself." And she urged Sage into a canter. She was unsaddling the horse when Ned came into the yard. She watched him hitch his horse by the trough and go into the house. *Probably going to report everything I did in town. I don't care.* She brushed Sage down and brought in some water and fresh hay. The horse nickered as she scratched Sage's nose. "I don't know what I'm in for when I see Father. You might be almost my only friend here."

She steeled herself and headed toward the house. Her father came out onto the porch when she was halfway there. *Uh-oh.*

"Catherine, I want to see you in my office *now*." He turned on his heel and went back inside.

She removed her hat and riding gloves, leaving them on the calling card table, and went through the parlor to the small alcove room Albert used as an office. It was barely large enough to hold his massive rolltop desk. Piles of paper and newspapers were situated on and off the desk and the one chair he'd managed to shoehorn in there.

Albert was seated at the desk, holding a serious-looking white envelope with a seal broken. "This came for you in the post."

She examined the address. "This was in my name and you opened it?" It was from a law firm in Tombstone.

"I felt I had to."

She ground her back teeth and read the letter. "Am I reading this right? They want me to go to their office on Wednesday next for the reading of Henderson's will? What does that have to do with me?"

Her father seemed to muster an astonished look. "How should I know? Maybe he left you some token."

"I barely knew the man, and what I did know, I didn't like."

"I'll go with you for the reading. And speaking of going into town, what was that all about this morning?"

She stared at him coldly. "Didn't Mr. Hadley fill you in?"

"He sure did. What on earth were you doing, going to the Chinaman area and the Bird Cage?"

She hesitated, then sighed. "I needed some information, and Jake was helping me. Ned the Nosy probably told you I was with Jake."

"And what kind of information did you need?"

"What kind of tea is in this tin." She pulled it out of her reticule.

He eyed the tin with a blank expression. "Why is that important? Where did you get that?"

"Because I was curious. Bill, the butler at

Henderson's house, gave it to me. He said Henderson had bought it intending it as a gift."

"What about the Bird Cage?"

"We didn't go inside. Jake wanted to talk to an employee, and we talked behind the building. Then we went for lunch and I came home."

He acted like he wanted to question further, but instead he wiped his hand across his mouth. "You know I don't approve of Spencer."

She paused. "I know, but I've experienced the person you did approve of." With that she turned and exited the office.

Chapter 16

Saturday morning, Jake was on his rounds gathering stories for the paper when he heard someone call his name. Turning, he saw John Monroe coming up behind him. "Wait up, Jake! I have a message from Cat for you."

Jake nodded toward the Oriental. "I'll buy you a beer." They walked through the swinging doors, and John took one of the tables in the far corner while Jake ordered two beers at the bar. Jake made his way through the tables and patrons and set the cold glasses down in front of them. "Now, what is the message?"

John took a swig of the beer and turned his eyes on Jake. "Cat wanted me to tell you she has been summoned to Lawyer Worthy's office for the reading of Henderson's will Wednesday next. Pa is going with her."

Jake drummed his fingers on the table. "I wonder what that means?"

John shook his head. "I don't rightly know. Something doesn't smell good all the way around. Cat has only been here a few months."

"But Henderson had designs on her from the very first. Why would he name her in his will? She resisted all his advances."

"I guess we'll find out next week. Cat said she wants to meet you for lunch at the restaurant on

Wednesday."

Jake paused. "Tell her I'll be there." They finished their beers and parted. Jake was worried, but he didn't know why.

****

Cat sat, barely breathing, in the upper floor lawyer's office. Seated before a large desk was Henderson's ranch foreman, along with the household staff—Bill and the housekeeper, the cook, and the maid. She and her father occupied the other two chairs. Mr. Gabe Worthy bustled into the office, carrying a folder of papers. He was a round little man with a bald head that he kept swiping with a handkerchief.

He made a great show of sitting down at his desk. Then he took out his pocket watch and thumbed it open. "I have eleven-thirty on the nose. Are we all assembled for the reading of Logan Henderson's will?"

Everyone nodded, and Cat picked at the lace on her sleeve. *I wish he would open a window. It's ungodly stuffy in here.* She pulled a fan from her reticule and lightly waved it in front of her face.

Worthy removed a brown envelope from the folder and unwound the string from the two cardboard buttons on the flap. He snapped out a stack of white legal paper and set it on the desk. Cat half heard the words about "sound mind" and "last will and testament." Then came the distribution of wealth. He read, "My money and property will be divided thusly. To my dear wife, Catherine." He paused when Cat gasped audibly. "I leave most of my money and the house and furnishings within. I also leave three acres of land on which the house and outbuildings are set, as well as the horses, carriages, wagons, and fowl. The remainder of the ranch acreage and cattle goes to my neighbor, Albert Monroe. To my household staff of butler Bill Grimes, housekeeper May Johnson, cook Hettie James, maid Jenny Simon, and foreman Toby Bates, goes a stipend of twenty-five dollars a month each, to be paid out of my general fund for as long as they work at the house. To this I set my seal this day, October fifteenth, eighteen eighty-three year of our Lord."

The women and foreman of the staff glanced at her sharply, and Bill looked at his shoes. Cat jumped up. "I'm sorry, I can't—"

Albert grabbed her by the arm. "Come with me now!" To the assembled, he said, "I'm afraid she's overcome. Excuse us." He pulled her out into the hallway and closed the door.

"Father," she said, a rasp in her voice, "I can't accept this. I never agreed to be his wife!"

He grasped her shoulders. "Catherine, listen. We can't help what he believed. Look what you've got—a grand home with servants, and probably a hundred and fifty thousand dollars. You're set for life!"

She was incredulous. "You don't understand, do you? My reputation is going to be in tatters, if it's not already. Having money is one thing, but being ostracized by polite society can be a very lonely wealth. I can't go back in there." She turned and ran down the stairs.

Albert stood at the entrance. "What am I going to tell those people?"

She huffed and glanced over her shoulder. "I don't care what you tell them." When he disappeared, she leaned against a post and started to cry. When she felt a presence and a hand on her shoulder, she jumped back and saw it was Jake. She didn't know where he'd come from, but she melted into his waiting arms and burst into tears anew.

"Cat. Cat, what's the matter?" he crooned.

Haltingly, she told him what had gone on in the lawyer's office. "With that will, he hurt me more that I ever thought. I'll be an outcast from here to Tucson. I want to sell the property."

Jake was silent for a moment. "Not yet. This may be an opportunity for us to find out what Henderson was up to."

"What?"

"We can search the house and see what we can turn up. This may be a way to answer a lot of questions."

"Does it matter anymore?"

"We may be able to lay to rest the questions Dara has about her sister."

Cat chewed on her lower lip. "I guess what's done is done. There's no helping me anymore. I may as well help her."

He pulled back and raised her chin. "You put way too much importance on the busybodies in this town. I'll stand by you no matter what, and I know others who will, too."

Albert and the others assembled by the lawyer were filing out the door, and Bill came up to her. "Miss Cat, I know this wasn't any of your doing. I'll be pleased to welcome you anytime you want to take a look at the house."

She managed a faint smile. "Thank you, Bill. I may be over today or tomorrow."

Jake spoke up. "We'll be over tomorrow."

Bill paused. "Yes, Mr. Spencer. I'll be expecting

both of you." He turned to Cat. "I'll talk to the staff. They need to realize you are in charge now." With that, he gave a slight nod of his head and went to join the others.

When Bill and the staff were out of earshot, Albert straightened from the post he was leaning against. "I have to say I'm not surprised to see you here, Spencer, now there's a money incentive to get in on. I'm guessing Cat told you what happened."

Jake's jaw tightened. "Yes, she told me. It doesn't matter a tinker's dam if she has money or not."

Cat glared at her father. "Don't you have things to do? Like looking over your new acreage and herd of cattle? And what about the hired hands Henderson had? Shouldn't they find out from you what's going on, rather than hearsay from the others who were here?"

Albert's fists opened and closed. "Girl, you have some sort of Virginia mule streak. Are you coming home with me or not?"

She opened her parasol. "Jake and I have a luncheon date. Will you come?"

Albert frowned. "I think I'll have a beer." He stomped through the swinging doors of the saloon next to them.

Jake offered his arm, and they picked their way across the street to the restaurant. As they found a seat at a table, some of the patrons turned and stared. Jake gave their order to the waiter.

Cat leaned in. "Looks like news is traveling like wildfire, judging on how some people are staring."

"Let them. You'll make it worse for yourself if you let them intimidate you. They love a good story, and so do I."

"You're not going to put this in the paper!"

Jake smirked. "I learned my lesson last time with you. However, this is the meatiest story in town right now."

She sighed. "I can't put this to rest soon enough. I want to get rid of the property and live at peace."

Their order came, and Cat ate quickly. She didn't like feeling like a sideshow freak with people gawking at them. As soon as Jake had paid for the meal, they walked out to find Albert waiting in the carriage. Cat felt the devil creep in and, before Jake could help her up, she turned and gave him a long kiss. Albert coughed lightly, but firmly. Jake didn't wipe the grin off his face as he boosted her up.

Cat waved. "I'll meet you at the property tomorrow morning."

He swept his hat off and gave a deep bow. "I'll be there."

Albert snapped the reins, and the horses made a fast clip-clop down the dusty street as Cat opened her parasol against the harsh midday sun.

Albert turned his attention on her. "I see you won't take my advice about Spencer."

She glared at him. "Your advice hasn't been too good so far. You don't understand that I have had it drummed into my head, from little on, that next to survival, having a good reputation is the most important thing. That now is in shambles, thanks to you and Henderson. I most certainly don't appreciate your going behind my back and making all those plans without my knowledge."

Albert sat back with a snort. "I was just trying to provide for you. Anyway, you kept seeing Jake behind my back."

"Fiddle-dee-dee! You always knew when I was going to see him. I never did anything without you knowing."

Albert stared straight ahead, and Cat figured the conversation was over for the time being. *All for the good. But it doesn't mean it's settled, by any means.* A cold icy silence built a wall between them.

Ilona Fridl

Chapter 17

Jake took a glance at the wall of gray clouds building up in the west. The breeze had turned cold, and he could feel in his bones that a November sleet storm could be coming. Riding to the Henderson ranch, he watched dust devils swirling the grasses, making them wave with abandon. A wet scent of moisture hit his nostrils. *Yep, we're in for a hard rain, at least.* As he turned into the property, he saw Cat's horse tied at the trough. He hitched his horse next to hers, then saw her on the porch.

Cat waved. "I just got here myself. Come in!"

Jake hurried up the steps, and they were met by Bill at the door. He gave Cat a slight bow. "I have talked to the staff, and they will cooperate with you. Anything you need, let me know."

"Thank you, Bill."

Jake turned to Cat. "We should look through Henderson's office to see if there was any outstanding debt before we do anything else."

"Yes, we need to see his office," Cat agreed and looked inquiringly at Bill.

"Yes, ma'am, this way." He led them through the parlor and into a small room in the back. The walls were lined with bookshelves holding all manner of books, newspapers, and magazines. The rolltop desk had a few envelopes and papers on top of the blotter.

The air smelled strongly of cigar smoke and old leather.

Cat glanced at Bill. "Where did Henderson keep his ledger?"

"In the top right-hand drawer of the desk. Here, I have the key for it."

He held out the key just as Jake opened the drawer. "The lock has been punched in." Jake picked up the desk lock from the inside of the drawer. "And there's no ledger here."

Bill looked surprised. "No one has been in this office since Mr. Henderson was killed."

Jake thought for a moment. "Was there anyone left here yesterday morning during the reading of the will?"

Bill shook his head. "No, Mr. Jake."

"Was the door locked while you were gone?"

"No, sir. There's no need to lock up. Nobody comes here."

Cat shook her head. "Seems like somebody did, unless one of the staff took it."

Bill pressed his lips together. "Everyone was in the carriage at the same time. Besides, it wouldn't do us any good. None of us can read."

"I'm sorry, Bill." Cat seemed contrite.

"No need, miss. You didn't know." He gave a slight bow and left the room.

Jake studied the lock and the drawer. "It looks like someone took a punch and hit the lock hard enough to break the wood at the top of the bolt." He found the broken piece of wood and fitted it to the split on the drawer. "They must have come in yesterday after the staff left for town."

Cat put her hands on her hips. "I wonder who and why?"

Jake saw the floor safe next to the desk and turned the handle. The safe was securely locked. "Henderson must have kept money in there, but we don't know if it was taken or not." He went to the door. "Bill!"

The butler returned. "Yes, sir?"

"Do you know the combination to this safe?"

"No, sir. Only Mr. Henderson knew."

Jake rubbed his chin. "We may have to take this to the blacksmith to open." He pulled several desk drawers open. Envelopes and papers were strewn on the bottom of each. "Looks like his correspondence was rifled through, too. Whoever took the ledger was afraid some information was going to be leaked."

Cat's eyes grew big. "I wonder if it was the person who killed him?"

Jake nodded. "I reckon that's a pretty good guess." He turned back to Bill. "Think, Bill. Did Henderson do anything in the last month or so out of the ordinary, besides buy the tea?"

Bill furrowed his brows. "Not that I know of. Except he started gathering elderberries from the stream side. He hasn't made elderberry wine in years."

"Did he do that after his wife died?"

Bill shook his head. "No, I don't think he did."

"Did he make the wine in the kitchen?"

"Hettie would kick up a fuss. He made it in a room in the barn." A sharp crack of thunder startled them all.

Jake turned to Cat. "Let's get the horses into the barn, and then we can check out the other rooms."

Cat smiled at Bill as she said, "Thank you for the information."

Bill gave a slight bow. "You're in charge now, Miss Cat." And he left the room.

Jake grabbed her hand and they hurried out the front door.

The horses were dancing, pulling at the tied reins. Jake undid them, and Cat opened the double doors to the barn as the rain began to fall. Jake half-ran, partially yanked by the two nervous steeds, as another streak of lightning split the air. Cat closed the barn and dropped the wood plank on the iron hooks that kept the doors together. The wind rattled the hinges, and a cold wet breeze blew under the timbers.

Jake stripped the horses of their saddles and found a couple of blankets to go over their backs. Now that they were inside, the animals quieted a bit, but Jake noticed Cat was shivering, and he took another blanket off the pile. "Here. Put this around you."

She did as she was told and jumped again when thunder rumbled in the distance. Jake lit a lantern and motioned to her. "Let's see if we can find that wine-making room Bill mentioned."

As the storm continued outside, they opened several shut doors. One was a storage room, one a tack room, and the last door they found led to steps going down to what appeared to be a cellar. Jake held up the lantern to what was a series of shelves with jars of many sizes nestled on them.

Cat glanced around. "This must be the root cellar."

A musty sweet odor hit Jake's nose as he turned to a table under the stairs. Elderberries on their stems were heaped next to a couple of vats under the table, with cloth and boards over the top of the vats Jake moved the light toward the table and saw a pile of elderberry leaves in a bowl. "Look at this."

Cat peered over his shoulder. "Why would he be

saving elderberry leaves?"

"We may have found his poison." Jake noticed a cloth hanging in the far corner beyond the table. He moved the cloth aside and saw corner shelves with some items. Along with ingredients for making wine, there was a rusty tin squeezed in at the back of a shelf. He fished it out and examined it. "Let me have the cloth on the far end of the table."

Cat took a couple of steps and grabbed it. Jake rubbed off the dirt and some of the rust, and Cat gasped. "That looks like the tea tin we already have."

Jake turned it over and at the bottom was an old pasted label which read: Lee Tang, Purveyor of Fine Herbal Teas, Tucson. "Seems like this was left over from his first wife, and he hid it out here." He worked at the rusted lid until it pulled off with a shower of tea and dirt. He poured some into his hand and studied it by the light. "This looks different from the tea we took to Lee Tang." He picked up one of the leaves. "Give me one of the elderberry leaves." As Cat did, he compared the two.

Cat leaned over and put her hand on his shoulder. He felt his body warm and was slightly distracted from her words. "From what I understand about poisons, elderberry leaves don't kill outright, but their effect builds up in the body."

Jake nodded. "That explains why his wife kept getting sicker. He must have made this for her every night."

He could feel Cat shudder. "He was planning to do that to me, too. But why? He got the land from his first wife. I didn't have anything he needed."

Jake thought a minute. "He probably thought you

would inherit some of the land from your father, if he married you."

Cat straightened and moved to a crate near the table, where she sat, putting her face in her hands. "I hate to think my father was unknowingly planning my life away."

The thought crossed Jake's mind that her father possibly did know, but he dismissed it. He put the lid on the tin. "I'm going to take this and show it to Dara. This is the proof she needs, proof she was right about Henderson."

Cat glanced at him. "I want you to put this in the paper. I want the town to know what he was. Then maybe I won't look so bad."

Jake stuffed the tin into his coat pocket and picked up the lantern. "If you're sure you want me to do that, I will."

She stood. "I'm sure."

Jake went ahead up the stairs, with Cat following. As he came out the door and moved into the main room of the barn, a gunshot knocked the lantern out of his hand. The oil splashed onto one of the beams and ignited a bale of hay below it. Flames billowed within seconds. At the sound of hoofbeats outside, he moved quickly to the stalls, calling back to a horrified Cat, "Get the doors open!"

She dropped the blanket and freed the double barn doors as Jake untied Henderson's three horses and gave them each a slap on the rump. The horses made a beeline to the outside. He untied his and Cat's horses and did the same, grabbing their saddles as he went.

The fire crawled up the beam and the hay continued to flame along the wall and into the mow, crackling and popping as it went. Cat screamed, "Jake!" as a burning plank from the loft came down behind him. A shower of sparks rained down like a spray from hell. Cat grabbed his arm, and they ran well away.

Toby and several of the hired men had come from the bunkhouse at the shout of "Fire!" from Bill, and they kept the horses from running away into the storm. The household staff watched from the back porch. Jake got hold of Cat's horse and his own and tied them near the house.

The storm passed soon, as though it had been sent to keep the fire from spreading, but there were puddles all around and the barn itself was an inferno by now. All they could do was watch it finish blazing and go into a heap of ashes.

Jake sought out Toby. "Did you see anyone in the yard before the barn caught fire?"

He swiped his handkerchief over his bald pate and shook his head. "I heard hoofbeats before I saw the fire, but I thought it was one of you."

"Didn't you hear a gunshot before?"

He studied the toe of his boot. "Yeah, but I thought it was a crack of thunder from the storm."

Jake asked the same of the household staff, but none had seen who it was. Bill said, "I saw someone jump the north fence, but I couldn't see who it was, from here."

Jake grabbed his saddle and put it on his horse. Cat came over and put her hand on his arm. "What are you doing?"

"I'm going to ride the north line of fence. With this rain, I should be able to find out where the one who shot at us went."

Cat tightened her lips. "I'm going with you."

"No. It's too dangerous."

She stood in his way. "We're in this together."

Jake ground his back teeth. "All right, but don't make me sorry I let you."

Cat saddled her horse while Jake waited, rebuking himself that he gave in too easily. Whoever was trying to kill him didn't care much about Cat being in the way. She rode to where he was waiting. "I'm ready."

They turned their horses to the road and went down the outside line of the fence. The clouds had broken, and the sun streamed over the saturated ground, reflecting brightly in the standing water. The horses' hooves made a soft plop-plop in the mud. Jake kept his eyes focused down by the fence until he pulled up and pointed. "It looks like he landed there." The prints of hooves were clear in the wet earth.

Cat visibly paled. "He's headed for Sugar Springs."

Jake started in the direction the hoofprints took. "I'm going to follow the tracks. Stay well behind me." Cat just nodded. As he rode, the route was unmistakable—it led right to the Sugar Springs ranch house. His heart was heavy for Cat. Someone there was the one who had nearly killed them. As he reached a line of cottonwood trees, a gunshot whizzed by him. He jumped off his horse and took cover behind a tree, drawing his pistol as he went. Glancing behind him, he noticed Cat had disappeared.

****

Cat dutifully followed about ten feet behind Jake, her heart getting heavier. Someone from Sugar Springs had tried to kill them in the barn. That must be the same one who killed Henderson. But who? And why? Her

161

stomach felt like a rock. Suddenly, she heard a shot and saw Jake jump off his horse. She quickly turned her horse around and circled into a copse of trees, where she dismounted and pulled her derringer out of her reticule. A couple more shots were fired while she quietly crept up behind the shooter. Raising her gun to point at the figure, she said, "Drop that gun! I'm aiming right at you!"

The figure whirled around and leaped onto his horse, taking off toward the yard at her father's ranch. The horse's white tail flashed like a beacon against the dark clouds in the eastern sky. *Flashed like a beacon?* Her mind immediately went back to the night of the masquerade. *That must be the horse I saw running down the dark street!*

She heard hoofbeats coming from the other way—Jake was chasing him. She ran to Sage, climbed on as fast as she could, and took off after them. By the time she came in sight of the house, Jake had the other man pinned down in the dirt, trading blows. Cat gasped and put her hand over her mouth. That was Ned Hadley!

Her father came out on the porch and fired his rifle into the air. "What's going on here?"

Cat rode next to them as Jake stood and pulled Ned up by his shirt front. "Your foreman shot at me in Henderson's barn and set it afire. He could have killed both me and Cat."

Albert grabbed Ned by the shoulder. "Is this true?"

Cat pointed at Ned. "He's the one who killed Henderson and shot Jake!"

All three men looked at her with astonishment, and her father rasped, "How do you know that?"

She set her jaw. "When I came around the building

that night, I saw a horse running away in the dark with a white tail flashing. When Ned took off just now, I noticed his horse's white tail flashing against the dark clouds, exactly the same."

Ned gnashed his teeth. "Why, you little hussy! I should—"

Albert shook him. "Shut up!"

Ned paled. "But, boss, you—" Albert's fist caught him in the face, and Ned went down.

Jake helped Cat off her horse and stood protectively by her. "I can take him in to the sheriff, if you'd like."

Albert glanced at Jake sharply. "No. I'll do this myself." He removed Ned's pistol. "Watch him while I saddle my horse."

Jake drew his gun and kept it trained at Ned. "All I want is a why."

Ned glared at Jake and spit on the ground. In a few minutes, Albert came riding up. "Mount up, Ned."

Cat spoke up. "Father, we should go with you. After all, we are the ones who witnessed his crimes."

Albert hesitated. Too long, in Cat's judgment. "All right, but stay behind us."

Cat and Jake remounted their horses. Albert and Ned were already halfway down the drive, and Jake moved closer to Cat. "That was a gutsy move you made back at the trees. I didn't know you carried a gun."

Cat patted her reticule where it swung over the saddle horn. "I learned how to shoot when I was fourteen. My uncle wanted me to be able to defend myself. There were many Union people who liked to harass Southerners."

Jake was quiet for a moment. "I'm sorry."

"What? Why?"

"Seems like there are always a lot of jackasses after a war." He paused. "Forgive me my language."

"I do forgive, but you're right." Cat suddenly thought of the barn fire at the ranch yard. She spurred her horse up to her father. "Father, will you stop at the—my ranch for a moment? I want to see about the barn fire."

Albert's eyebrows raised, but he nodded. "We can."

They turned their horses into the drive, and the black smoke of the ruined barn came into view. Cat trotted Sage to where Toby and the three hired men stood watching for sparks. "Toby, will you and the hands make straw beds in the carriage house for the horses until we can rebuild the barn?"

Toby spit on the ground. "You givin' the orders now?"

Cat ground her back teeth. "Yes, I own this place. You take orders from me."

"Your father owns the pasture land and the cattle. Shouldn't we be takin' orders from him?"

Cat said sharply, "Mr. Bates, the land we're standing on is *my* concern. Everything on it is under *my* control. Now, if my father wishes for you to take care of the cattle on his part of the ranch, that's up to him. But you were also hired to take care of the outbuildings. I'm willing to pay the hired hands twenty-five a month as well, if they're willing to stay on."

Toby's face turned umber. "You'd pay these coyote baits the same as me? I won't stand for it!"

Cat felt more strength than she ever did in her life. "Then you can pack up and leave. I'm sure I can find someone else for the job."

Toby looked like he wanted to hit something. He took his hat off and slammed it to the ground. "All right, *Miss Cat*, I'll do it."

Cat turned Sage around and went to the house, where the staff was watching from the porch. May, the housekeeper, stepped forward. "I really must protest, Miss Monroe. We're being paid no more'n the riffraff?"

Cat was at her wit's end. "The same goes for all of you. If you're unhappy, leave. Remember, I can replace any one of you."

Bill, who was standing in front of the others, gave her a slight smile and a bob of his head as the staff turned and went inside.

Cat urged her horse back to the party waiting for her. Her father and Ned watched her, goggle-eyed, and Jake, although he wasn't laughing, had merriment coming out of every pore.

Albert pushed his hat back. "My word, Cat, I didn't know you had it in you to cow those tough hombres. I have to admit, you can run things. You got a backbone, girl."

Albert and Ned turned their horses and headed toward town. As Cat and Jake followed, Jake moved his horse next to hers again. "Bravo, Cat!" he said low. "But your payments aren't fair."

Cat smiled. "I realize that. But they will have to come to me if they have a complaint, and I could be persuaded to give them a raise. And the hired men will still think they are making as much as anyone else."

"How did you learn to be such a business tycoon?"

"By listening to my uncle when he talked to Ben at the dinner table, back in Virginia."

Jake shook his head and chuckled. Cat was gaining

more confidence in her abilities every day, and she felt satisfied for the first time in her life.

Chapter 18

Cat was deep in thought as the group dismounted and tied their horses in front of the sheriff's office. Albert and Jake had their guns trained on Ned as they escorted him into the building with Cat trailing behind. The sheriff looked up from his desk. "What is this?"

Albert holstered his gun. "We believe this is the one who killed Logan Henderson."

The sheriff's mouth gaped. "But this is your foreman. What proof do you have?"

Jake and Cat filled him in on the events of the day, as well as what Cat had noticed after the shooting at the masquerade.

The sheriff listened carefully. "That's pretty strong evidence." He glanced at Ned. "What do you have to say about that?"

Ned glared at Albert. "I want a lawyer," he growled.

Cat saw her father's forehead furrow, and she wondered why. He seemed worried about something. The sheriff led Ned away, and the three others stepped outside. Jake checked his pocket watch. "How about a bite to eat? My treat."

They picked their way across the street through the mud and wiped their shoes on the straw mat provided at the door of the restaurant. As soon as they sat at one of the tables in the post-meal emptiness, a waiter came up to them. "Yes, sir?"

Jake studied the slate board where the menu was listed. "Does the beef stew sound good to you?" Albert and Cat nodded. Jake continued, "We'll have that plus bread and coffee."

The waiter took their order to the kitchen. Cat eyed both Jake and her father, both of whom seemed uncomfortable. "Father, please. Jake has helped me immensely since I arrived here. Can't you at least admit that?"

Albert scowled. "If only he wasn't a Spencer."

Jake shook his head. "I can't help where I was born. I do love your daughter and want to court her."

"Now that she has money, eh?"

Cat slammed her hand on the table. "He loved me before this happened. Or have you discounted all I've said?"

Albert was silent, then sighed. "I guess I'll give you my blessing. Lord, I have a headstrong daughter."

Their food arrived, and they ate in relative silence for the rest of the meal. Jake paid the tab, and they left the restaurant. As Jake stepped off the sidewalk, he said, "I'll go get the horses. Wait here," and he came back leading the four horses. Albert mounted his and took the reins of Ned's. Jake went to boost Cat onto her horse, and she put her arms around his neck and kissed him soundly. Her father cleared his throat and she stopped, a grin splitting her face.

She put her hand on Jake's cheek. "I'll see you."

His intense eyes were on her. "You bet you will." He helped her up onto the saddle.

"I'll be in town tomorrow to order lumber for the barn. I'll find you." She and her father turned their horses to the road out. "Father, I think I should move into the house at the ranch, since I'm responsible for it now."

"I need you at Sugar Springs."

"Why? I don't do anything there. And you won't be so far away."

Albert looked like he had a bad taste in his mouth. "All right."

"And what about my idea that Henderson's hired men should take care of that herd of cattle for you?"

"Yes, yes. That would be fine." Her father seemed distracted. All the way back to Sugar Springs he gave short answers to her statements and questions.

When they dismounted in front of the house, Cat scratched Sage's nose. "May I have Sage? I've grown fond of this mare."

"Uh, yes, of course. Will you unsaddle Ned's horse? And tell Peterson to come into my office."

Cat led the horse around the back of the corral to the bunkhouse, where the hired men were busy unsaddling their horses after looking in on the cattle herd. Cat found the tall Dane. "Karl! My father wants to see you in his office."

He tipped his hat. "Yes, ma'am."

She led the horse into its stall in the barn and pulled the saddle off. After brushing down the animal, she got some hay from the loft and put it into the food trough, then grabbed the bucket and went to the well behind the barn. As she was pumping the water, her eyes went to the burn pit where they disposed of excess brush. Something black with red sections rested at the bottom of the ashes. Cat set the bucket down and went to inspect it. It was a book of some kind. It was damp, and the ashes caked around it were like gray mud. *The rainstorm must have put the fire out. But what is it, and why were they trying to burn it?*

She brushed it off the best she could and opened it. It looked like a ledger. The pages were burned around the edges, but she could make out some of the entries. Then she gasped. On one page she saw wages and names listed for Henderson's staff. *This is the missing ledger. But what is it doing here? I wonder if Ned took it when the staff was in town for the reading of the will? Why on earth did he do all these things? I don't see how he had anything to gain.*

She tucked the ledger under her arm and took the water to the horse. When she was ready to go to the house, she slipped the ledger into her saddlebag and went to pack a few things. Karl and Albert were at the door when she came down.

Karl grinned and shook Albert's hand. "I know this ranch like the back of my hand. You can count on me."

Albert nodded. "Good. Tell the men what happened and that you're in charge now." As Karl left, Albert turned to Cat. "That's all you're taking?" He stared incredulously at the small satchel.

"I plan to stay overnight tonight. I'll return with the wagon tomorrow."

He put his hand on her cheek. "I'll miss you around here."

She patted it. "I'm not that far away. I could use all the help I can get when I rebuild the barn."

He smiled. "I'll be there. Cat, I'm very proud of you."

She kissed his cheek. "Thank you, Father. That means a lot to me." She went down the porch steps, slung the satchel's handles around the saddle horn, and climbed up. She waved. "See you sometime tomorrow!" Cat set off, feeling like singing.

****

Jake wandered to the Bird Cage and sat down at one of the faro tables in the saloon. He pitched a dollar on the table. "A stack of chips." The dealer obliged and started flipping cards. After a couple of losses, Jake spied Dara at a far table, talking to some of the gamblers. He rose and walked through the cigar smoke fog to where she stood. "May I talk to you outside?"

She glanced at the gamblers. "I'll be back in a few minutes, boys." They walked out the side door, and as Jake leaned against one of the posts she asked, "Did you and Cat come up with something?"

Jake removed the rusty tin from his jacket pocket and told her how they'd found it. "I thought you'd like to see proof that your suspicions were correct." He showed her the elderberry leaves mixed in with the tea.

Tears rolled down her cheeks. "Thank you. I guess Henderson got what was coming to him. I just wish the finger on the trigger had been mine."

Jake gave her his handkerchief. "We found that out, too. It was Ned Hadley."

She put her hand over her mouth. "What?"

Jake went on to tell her about the barn fire and capture. "I still don't know why he did it. It doesn't make any sense."

She silently gazed at the tin. "This puts my mind at rest. I finally got my answer." She kissed his cheek, handed the tin back to him, and went inside again.

Jake headed to the newspaper office and sat down at his desk, took a composition book out of his desk drawer, and began to write. Harvey wandered over. "You got a story, Jake?"

"Got a humdinger of a one. Just wait till you see this." He set the tin in front of him for inspiration.

****

The next morning, Cat tied her horse in front of the lumber dealer's establishment on Fremont Street. She went into the small front alcove and saw a heavyset man seated at a desk. He was in his shirtsleeves and wearing a blue visor perched on top of his balding head. The air was filled with the smell of fresh-cut wood, and she could hear a steam-generated saw buzzing in the backyard. He looked up and seemed surprised to see her. "Are you here for something, miss?"

"Yes." She took some notepaper out of her reticule. "I need an order of lumber to build a barn with a loft. Here are the dimensions." She spread the paper out in front of him.

He took a book out of a drawer and checked the tables. "We can have your order cut and ready by Monday next. Do you have a way of transporting it to the site?"

"How many wagons do you think I'll need?"

"Probably four, with long beds."

"All right. I'll pay when I pick it up. How much for the wood and the hardware? That is included, is it not?"

"Yes, we offer a building package, everything included." He pulled out a composition book with prices in it. He ran a grimy finger down one of the columns. "That will be one hundred and thirty dollars."

Cat peered at the book. "Excuse me. That is for one with larger dimensions." She pointed to the line below. "That is the size I need."

He frowned. "Wrong one. All right, miss, that's one hundred and fifteen. Now, who's going to cosign for this?"

She paused. "You don't understand. This is my land, and I'll pay in cash."

He shook his head. "For that amount of money, we need a cosigner for a woman."

She put her fists on her hips. "May I speak with the owner?"

"You are. Now either you find someone to cosign for you or say good day."

Cat wanted to cry, but she knew that would be disastrous. "Well, you start on the order, and I'll come back with someone."

"Not until you get a cosign." He handed her the notepaper.

Cat huffed and turned on her heel. "I'll be back." She marched out the door and beat her hand on the hitching post. Climbing on Sage, she went to find Jake. The newspaper office loomed as she rode up the street. Inside, the smell of ink permeated the air, and the scream of metal parts and a clinking sound came from the back room. "Is Jake Spencer here?" she asked a man at a desk.

He jerked a grimy thumb toward the back. "He's helping at the press."

The massive press, made of iron and wood, stood royally in the middle of the room, with men attending it. The inker stood at the ready with two round blotters to spread on the cuts and letters. The pressman pulled a lever and a metal block came down, pressing the paper onto the inked form. Jake was pulling off the paper and putting a clean sheet over it. He grinned. "We're about finished with today's edition. Sit at my desk, and I'll be out in ten minutes."

She did as she was told and watched the pendulum clock on the wall ticking out the time. Cat was weary of heart and spirit. Too much to take, between having all this responsibility thrust on her and running into brick walls just because she was a woman. A tear gathered at the corner of her eye and trickled down her cheek.

Jake came out from the back room, toweling ink off his hands, and she hastily dashed the tear away. His face registered concern. "Cat, what's the matter?"

She bit on her lip. "I need a cosigner to get the materials for the new barn."

He nodded. "I had a feeling you were going to run into that trouble. I'll help you with that." He called out to the man at the desk. "Harvey, I'm going out for a while." The man waved his hand absently. Cat rose and went with Jake. "Did you go to the lumber merchant on Fremont?" Cat indicated she did. "Ride over, and I'll meet you in a few minutes."

Cat stayed on her horse until she saw Jake striding up the sidewalk. She dismounted and tied the reins to the hitching post. He put his arm around her shoulders, and she quivered at his touch. "Ready?" he asked.

She steeled herself. "Yes."

The balding man was still at his desk and looked up. "Jake! Good to see you, boy!" He stood to shake Jake's hand. Then he noticed Cat. "Oh, you're back."

Jake waved toward Cat. "She's what I want to see you about, Otto. I want to cosign the payment for the building materials."

"Are you good for it?"

"She has more money than I do. But if you need a

174

cosign, I'll do it."

Otto hesitated. "It's our rules, you understand."

"I know. You won't be flim-flammed."

Otto took a sheet of paper out of his desk drawer. "Let's see, if I remember, it was for the one-hundred-and-thirty-dollar package."

Cat grimaced. "No. It was the one-hundred-and-fifteen."

He frowned. "Oh, yes, you're right."

He's trying to flim-flam me. She pursed her lips in annoyance.

Otto completed the form. "Do you have any good faith money?"

She took ten dollars in coins out of her reticule. "Will this do?"

He made note of it on the form. "Come in Monday next with four long-bed wagons."

When they went outside, she slumped against a post. "Now where can I get four long-bed wagons and four teams of horses?"

"I know of a livery stable that hires to construction crews. I'll help you arrange that. They may be reluctant to hire to a woman, as well. I'm sorry."

She put her hand on his shoulder. "I am grateful for your help." She moved to get back on her horse, but paused. "Jake, I found Henderson's ledger."

His eyes narrowed. "Where was it?"

She related to him how she'd found it. "It's still in my saddlebag. Is there a place we can look at it in privacy?"

He thought for a moment. "The only place with privacy is my apartment. Do you want to ruin your reputation further?"

"It's already shot. I'll meet you there." She climbed up and turned her horse to the road east. She tied the reins in the front of the building, pulled the saddlebags off, and sat on the steps to wait for Jake.

When he arrived, they went inside, where he pulled two chairs to the table. "Let's see what you have."

She removed the charred ledger from the bag and set it in front of him. "I think the storm yesterday put the fire out before it could burn the pages fully."

Jake carefully opened it, sending burnt flakes fluttering to the table surface. "Something is in here that someone didn't want brought to light."

She and Jake studied the first few pages they could read. She pointed at several entries. "Henderson put the reasons for the payments to him and the out payments, except on certain lines."

Jake nodded. "I noticed that. Let's see if we can find a page that says who the payments are from."

They paged through several months of records until they found one of the mysterious lines contained a faint "roe" coming out of a burnt edge. Cat put her finger under it. "Could that mean my father or brother was paying a hundred dollars a month for something?"

Jake studied it. "Well, you may be jumping to conclusions. We can't tell who the other non-noted payments were for."

"I wonder if Ned was indebted to Henderson for some reason but didn't want anyone to know. It would make sense if he was paying him off and killed him to save himself one hundred a month."

Jake shook his head. "I know your father has money, but I wouldn't think he was paying Ned that much a month."

Cat shrugged. "Maybe that was the reason Ned killed Henderson."

"But why would he shoot me? Henderson was down when a bullet came my way."

"He thought you saw him?"

Jake sighed. "It could be. We're just snatching at straws here."

Cat's head felt ready to explode, and she burst into tears. "I don't know anything anymore." She put her face in her hands and sobbed. Jake stood next to her and drew her gently into an embrace. She cried her misery onto his shoulder while he soothed her. "I wish I'd never come here." She sniffed and pulled away. She searched through her reticule for a handkerchief.

Jake handed her his and put his arm around her. "I, for one, am very happy you came here. I think you're a remarkable woman, Cat." His smile and his eyes told her the truth.

She snuggled into the warmth and strength of his embrace again. She felt so protected and so loved. As they stood there, locked together, a change came over her. Her chest tightened, and a tingling started through her body. Her breath caught in her throat. She suddenly pulled back, and Jake gazed at her with that intense expression she had seen several times. She caressed his whisker-rough cheek. "Jake?"

With a wordless answer, he locked his lips to hers in a thorough kiss. Honey velvet rolled down her skin, and everywhere they touched was on fire. She had her arms around his neck, and he smoothed his hands down the contours of her body. She shuddered as he did so. He tightened his body onto hers, and through the thin material of her riding skirt, she was pressed against a hardening swell in his groin. "I want you," he growled.

Her intimate parts were bursting with moisture, and she ground into him without thinking. She should run away and say no, but her body wasn't cooperating with her. They were both panting like dogs lying in the sun.

Jake kissed down her neck to her throat, where he gave her a caress with his tongue. She was losing her sense of reason and tore her fingers into his back. Jake moaned with her. He loosened the top few buttons on her shirt, running his hand over the soft mounds of her bosom that padded above her corset. She felt more pleasure than she'd ever understood a body could take. Without knowing how she got there, she was reclined on his bed with her corset cover off and Jake unhooking the front. One breast was freed, and he kissed the tip of the nipple. An erotic shock jerked her body.

Cat was way over her head now, and all sense of propriety was fast disappearing. She moved her fingers down his arms, and he shuddered. She felt some satisfaction that her touch could make him feel what she was experiencing.

Jake tugged on the fasteners on the side of her riding skirt, and the cloth was soon discarded. The ties of her drawers were the only thing in his way now. The cool air hit her body with a rush, but soon all was heated again as he divested himself of his clothes.

Cat lightly put her hand on the bulge in his drawers, straining at the buttons. He moaned as he let the monster loose. Cat gasped as she gripped the soft silky steel. He shuddered again and climbed on top of her. The prickle of his body hair delighted her, and the hardness pressed against her intimate opening made her vibrate. He moved, and her body seemed to sing.

They kissed, their tongues entwined, as he pushed his way into her opening, his flesh tearing hers. She cried out, but the pain gave way to the delight of him inside her. He rocked to and fro. Her core tightened like a clock spring until she could stand it no more. Suddenly that spring released and her limbs were not her own. Minutes—hours?—of pleasure coursed through her. She became aware of clutching Jake, her arms and legs entwined around him. A peaceful glow radiated from every pore.

Slowly, he extracted himself and sat back on the bed. "Oh, Cat, I'm so sorry."

She stirred languidly. "Sorry for what? That was the most wonderful thing I've ever experienced."

He sighed. "I know how important reputation is to you."

She smirked. "It was wrecked anyway. Might as well stop pretending."

He sat there lost in thought. "Marry me, Cat. I can't live without you."

Her heart jumped a beat. "You're asking me before you talk to my father?" Then she laughed. "Still thinking about propriety, aren't I? Yes, I want to marry you!" Suddenly, she was uncomfortable with no clothes, and she pulled the sheet around her, her cheeks heated. "We'd better get dressed."

Jake kissed her forehead and bundled his clothes to the other side of the room while she put on hers by the bed. Cat stood in front of his shaving mirror and smoothed back her rumpled hair. Jake came up behind her, slipped his arms around her waist, and kissed her ear. Shock waves went through her body. "I love you," he said low, stirring the wisps of hair on her neck.

She turned, and the wound on her opening gave a stinging twinge. She gritted her teeth. "I don't know how I'm going to ride home."

Jake gave her a look of concern. "Stay at a hotel tonight."

She checked her coins. "Looks like I have enough for one night. Could you bed down Sage while I check in? I'll meet you in the dining room at six."

He nodded. "That will give me time to stop at the newspaper office. I don't want Harvey to know I wasn't doing my job."

She put on her hat and picked up the ledger and her reticule. "This is going to stay with me." She patted his cheek and hurried down the steps. In a couple of blocks, the hotel loomed ahead. How much had changed since she first came to Tombstone! That August day seemed a million years ago. As she walked into the lobby, Ed was at the desk, and she greeted him warmly.

"What can I do for you, Miss Monroe?"

"I'd like a room for the night. I have some business here in town tomorrow, and I thought I'd save a trip home." She paid for a room and signed the register. "How is Edna these days?"

He grinned. "She's doing fine. She loves the little house in town we just moved into. You'll have to stop and see her. We live in the second house down on the south side of Fourth and Safford."

She nodded. "Thank you, I will. Could you have a bathtub with hot water sent to my room?"

"Yes, Miss Monroe. Right away."

Soon she was luxuriating in a tub, with lavender-scented soap. The steam caressed her face as it wafted up. So much to think about. Cat's world wasn't as ordered as she tried so hard to achieve. She surely wasn't the paragon of virtue her aunt and uncle had raised her to be. Somehow, it didn't bother her as much as she'd thought it would. Jake came into her thoughts, and she smiled. *I came here to find a father, and I also found the love of my life.*

She gave the sponge a final squeeze over her shoulders and stood up. Grabbing the towel from the stand beside her, she stepped out of the tub. She wished she had a change of clothes with her, but this would have to do. At the vanity, she managed to pin her hair into order and pinched her cheeks for color.

A knock at the door came with the announcement, "Miss Monroe, a Mr. Spencer is here."

Cat turned and called, "Tell him I'll be right down." She took the ledger and stored it under the mattress. When she was satisfied that no one could tell where it was stashed, she left the room.

Jake waited for her at the bottom of the stairs and beamed when he saw her. Swinging her around in an embrace, he said, "I missed you."

As an answer, she planted a kiss on his lips, then pulled back and smiled. "I missed you, too."

They were headed to the dining room when a host stopped them. "I'm sorry, but you must be in dinner dress to dine here."

Cat put her hand on Jake's arm before he could protest. "That's all right. We can go elsewhere."

They walked to the little restaurant down the street and sat at one of the tables. Jake ordered for them and sat back in the chair. "Where is the ledger?"

Cat checked around and said so only Jake could hear. "It's in a safe place." She shifted her gaze out the window and noticed a figure walking by in the dim light of the lamppost. "What is my father doing in town?"

Jake glanced in the direction she was nodding toward. "That does look like Albert. Who knows? He doesn't seem to be searching for you."

Cat watched as the man got on his horse and rode out. "Maybe he had some business he had to take care of."

Their order came, and Cat put any thought of her father out of her mind.

Chapter 19

Jake and Cat started back to the hotel after he paid for their dinner. They were walking past the sheriff's office when a commotion from inside caught their attention. A man came out and pushed by them. Jake, ever the reporter, went inside, and Cat followed. "What happened here?" He took out his paper and pencil.

The sheriff scowled. "Well, I guess you've got the scoop. Ned Hadley seems to have been poisoned. I just sent the deputy to get Doc."

Jake heard a gasp behind him. "Poisoned?" Cat exclaimed.

"Where were you two, by the way?"

Jake pointed down the street. "We were having dinner for the past hour. Ask anyone there. Anyway, we were the ones who brought him in. Why would we kill him?"

The sheriff hesitated. "I guess you're right."

Jake turned to Cat. "I want to stay here and get the story, if it's all right with you."

She nodded. "I'd like to know what happened, too."

Feet pounded on the walk outside, and Doc and the deputy tore into the office. Doc nodded his head toward the back. "There?"

The sheriff jerked his thumb. "Cell door is open."

In a few minutes, Doc came back carrying a half-lit

cigar in his handkerchief. "I have to take this to my office to check, but I think there's arsenic soaked into the end of the cigar. When he lit it and started drawing on it, he got enough poison to kill him."

The sheriff exploded. "How in the name of Hades did he get a cigar and matches? Mort!"

The deputy had his hat in a shaky hand. "I don't know, Sheriff. No one has come to visit him this evening, and I don't think he had it when I removed the dinner tray."

"Someone must have passed it to him between the bars. Go and see if you can find anything outside the window."

Jake was quickly writing all this down. He turned to Cat. "I'll walk you back to the hotel, and then I'm going to the newspaper office to give them the story."

They hurried to the building and up the stairs to her room. When she opened the door, she cried out. The contents of her saddlebags were strewn all over the floor. Her eyes grew large. "The ledger!" She turned to the bed and raised the mattress. Tugging out the burnt book, she sighed in relief. "Whoever did this must have been looking for the ledger. Nothing is missing."

Jake was torn about leaving her there by herself. "Do you have your gun with you?"

She patted her reticule. "I always have it with me."

"Good. Take it out and leave it handy. You may have to use it." He headed toward the door. "I'll be back in less than an hour. Hide the ledger again."

Jake stopped by the desk on the way out. "Ed, can you keep an eye on the door to Cat's room while I'm out? Don't let anyone go in there."

"I'll try, Jake."

He flew down the sidewalk, pushing through groups of drunks and strollers until he got to the office. Harvey was finishing up the evening's printing when Jake slapped the notes onto his desk. "Ned Hadley was poisoned at the jail. Can't stop to talk now. It's in my notes."

"Where are you going?"

"Got to help a friend." Jake shot out the door, leaving Harvey sputtering behind him. He dashed into the livery stable. "Pete, are you here?"

Pete came out from the back. "Hey, Jake. What do you want?"

"I need to hire a rig now. And tie Cat's horse to the back of it. Don't bother with the saddle."

Pete put a harness one of the carriage horses while Jake hauled the saddle into the back of the rig. As Jake pressed a number of coins into Pete's palm, the livery man scratched his head. "Any reason you're in such of an all-fired hurry?"

Jake jumped into the driver's seat and took the reins. "Yes." He snapped the reins, and the horse took off into the night. When he arrived at the hotel, he tied the reins and strode inside, took the stairs two at a time, and knocked at Cat's door. "Cat. It's me. Jake."

Cat opened the door. She had put her belongings back into the saddlebags. "No one came looking for anything."

Jake pointed to the bed. "Grab the ledger and let's go."

"Where are we going?"

"Back to your home. Now hurry!"

She retrieved the book and stuffed it into her saddlebag. Jake took the saddlebag and threw it over his shoulder while she grabbed her reticule and followed him out. He stopped by the desk.

Ed came out. "What is it, Jake?"

"Cat's leaving, just to let you know, but there's no reason to tell anyone else if they come looking for her." He flipped a coin to Ed. Helping Cat onto the rig, he then untied the reins and climbed up beside her and snapped the reins.

Cat gazed at him with eyes wide. "Why are we leaving?"

He ground his teeth. "Whoever is searching for the ledger didn't find it here. I'll wager a week's pay they went to your house to look for it." Jake worried that he was driving her into danger, but there was danger in leaving her in town all alone, too. As long as she was with him, he could protect her.

In the light of the waxing moon, Jake glanced at Cat, who held on grimly but said nothing. *She must be scared of what she might find, too.* In a while, the dim glow of the Henderson house loomed in the distance. Jake turned the horse into the drive, and Cat gasped out, "Father!" Albert's horse was tied at the post.

As they ascended to the porch, Bill came out with a lantern. "Miss Monroe, Mr. Spencer, I wasn't expecting you tonight."

Cat drew herself up in front of him. "Why is my father here?"

"He told me you were staying in town at a hotel and asked him to take a few things to you."

Cat put her hand to her forehead. "But how—?" She dashed inside and up the stairs, with Jake on her heels. Cat threw open the door to her room and caught her father going through her wardrobe. "What are you doing?"

Albert spun around and was at a loss for words. His face hardened, and he rasped, "Where is it?"

She put her fists on her hips. "Where is what?"

Albert came over and gripped her shoulders. "You know very well what. I know you took it."

"How?" He shook her slightly, and Jake made a move toward him. "Stop, Jake. Father, how do you know?"

"It was in the burn pit when the storm hit. I questioned the hands, and you were the only one around there when it disappeared."

"I thought Ned had taken it and burned it for some reason. Where are you in this little theater play, Father?"

Albert paused. Jake thought Albert had said more that he should have. Albert picked up an atomizer off the vanity and threw it across the room. It shattered, and the smell of lavender hit their noses. "My own daughter comes to town and ruins everything!" He strode out of the room.

Jake and Cat followed him downstairs and watched from the porch as Albert mounted his horse and rode toward Sugar Springs. Bill appeared at the door. "I have some hot tea and cakes in the parlor."

Cat nodded. "Thank you. We'll be there in a minute." He inclined his head and stepped back inside. She blew out a breath. "At least he didn't see the ledger in the rig."

Jake hopped off the porch. "I'm going to get it right now." He returned with her saddlebags. "I'll bed Sage down. Meet you inside." Cat relieved him of the bags, and he walked Sage to the carriage house, carrying the saddle. All the while he was wondering what the hell Albert and Henderson had cooked up. Why did Ned Hadley kill Henderson and shoot him? Why was Hadley poisoned? And who did that? Something in that ledger held the key.

Back in the house, Jake found Cat on a chair at the small table, with the ledger open in front of her. Jake poured himself some tea and sat on a chair beside her. "Find anything?"

"I've been looking into when these mysterious payments from my father started. It seems it goes back three years." She pushed the book in front of him. "This is the first entry I found."

Jake studied it carefully. "Something was erased on that line. Could you get a pencil for me?"

Cat disappeared into the office and came back with one. "What are you going to do?"

He lightly rubbed the graphite over the line and a faint word of "water" came out like a photographic plate. He sat back. "Water? Why was Albert paying Henderson for water? Your father has the spring."

Cat shook her head. "It means something very important to my father if he wants this book so badly."

Jake was getting a dark picture of Albert, but he didn't want to alarm Cat until he had more proof. "Let's find a place to hide the ledger that will be safe."

Cat thought for a moment. "How about putting it back in the drawer in the desk where it came from?"

Jake furrowed his brow. "Wouldn't that be too easy to find?"

"No one would expect it to be there. Did you ever read *The Purloined Letter* by Edgar Allen Poe? Hide it in a place where it should be."

Jake gave a slow smile. "You know, that may work." He kissed Cat on the forehead. "Put it there, and I'll get Bill to help me load the safe onto the rig. Maybe we can find some information in there."

After they had lugged the heavy safe to the back porch and hefted it into the rig, Jake turned to Bill. "Watch out for Miss Monroe, will you?"

Bill nodded. "I can hear anyone coming to the house, even from my room." He went back inside, and Jake embraced Cat.

"Come into town tomorrow. I'll be at the blacksmith's, next to the livery stable." As an answer Cat kissed him thoroughly. Jake's groin tightened, remembering her sweet warm flesh. Reluctantly, he pulled back and climbed into the driver's seat. "Be careful coming into town tomorrow."

Cat waved. "I will. I love you!" As he snapped the reins, she turned and watched him go from the porch. A blend of joy and worry colored his thoughts.

It was late when he took the rig back to the livery stable, but Pete was waiting for him. "Pete, could you help me get this safe off the rig?"

Pete snorted. "What'd you do? Rob somebody?"

"Very funny. No, but I have to get it opened." They eased it down onto its wheels, and Jake pushed it to the blacksmith's shop next door. The business was closed, but the small house next to it still had a lantern lit. Jake pounded on the door. "Cleve! Can I see you a minute? It's Jake!"

A big burly blond man opened the door. "What brings you out at this hour?"

"I want you to open a safe for me tomorrow, and I don't want to haul it up to my room."

Cleve yawned and lifted a ring of keys from a hook beside the door. "We can wheel it to the side door."

After it was locked inside, Jake said, "How long do you think it will take to open?"

"Judging by the hinges on the door, about half a day to cut off."

"Thanks, Cleve. I'll be over after lunch." Jake hoped they would find the answer inside.

****

Cat rode into town after a sleepless night. So much was going on inside her head with the ledger, the safe, her father, and Jake, she barely knew what to think anymore. She had spent the morning making sure the hands knew how to raise a barn. Toby was cordial since he had negotiated with her for an increase in pay. She didn't know how receptive her father would be to the idea of his hands lending their help. Maybe Jake could put an ad in the paper for her.

The blacksmith's shop announced itself by the smell of coal smoke and a loud clanging. Jake leaned against the frame of the open double doors, and her heart jumped when she saw him. Cat tied Sage at the post on the street, took off the saddlebags, and went to stand next to Jake. She tried to ignore the tingling in her body.

Jake turned to her and grinned. "Cleve has the safe almost opened."

She watched as the blacksmith drove a wedge into the space between the frame and the door on the side where the hinges used to be. The combination lock had been knocked off and the mechanism destroyed. Cleve and his assistant pried up on the wedges, and the safe gave a moan. A wedge was driven in on the other side, and the door popped over to expose the bolt. Cleve put a chisel on the bolt and gave a mighty blow with the sledgehammer. Cat heard the clatter of a metal plate inside, and they were able to pry the door off.

As Cleve was cleaning the wreckage of the door out of the interior, Cat and Jake went to inspect the contents. There were several large envelopes and folders tucked into the cubbyholes. Cat held her saddlebag open, and Jake transferred the contents to it.

Jake turned to Cleve. "How much for the work?"

"Twelve dollars, if you let me have the safe for scrap."

Cat checked in her reticule. "I only have seven with me."

Jake gave her five coins. "You can pay me back," he said with a leer that made her toes curl. "Let's go get the long-bed wagons and teams hired before we look at the papers."

Cat flipped the saddlebags over Sage, Jake went to the livery stable to get his horse, and together they made their way to the large yard that rented out construction equipment. Jake had no trouble securing the wagons and teams, and Cat realized there were a lot of things she wouldn't be able to do without him. That rankled, but it made her grateful she had him.

Cat and Jake mounted up again. He glanced at her. "Let's go to my apartment and see what you have for papers."

They were two blocks away when Cat noticed a tall blond man leaning on one of the posts outside the building. She pulled up sharp. "Jake, stop. That's my father's new foreman, Karl."

Jake turned his horse into a loading area between

the buildings. "Follow me!" He opened his coat and unbuttoned his shirt. "Give me the envelopes and folders."

Cat did so, and he stuffed them into his clothes and closed his coat. Cat pressed her lips. "Are you going to try to get those past him?"

Jake grinned. "That's the idea. Now, if he asks for your saddlebags, give them to him."

They casually rode toward the apartment, and as they dismounted Karl confronted them. He pushed his hat back with his thumb. "Miss Monroe, Cleve tells me you put the papers from the safe into your saddlebags. Your father wants them."

Cat stared. "What would my father want with my saddlebags?"

"He said to tell you there was some business from Mr. Henderson that he needed."

She swung her bags off the horse. "I'll give this to you only if you don't open them until you see my father."

Karl just grunted. The bags were across his horse's back before she could speak again, and in no time they were watching him ride away.

Jake grabbed her hand. "That should buy us some time to look at these."

Soon they had the envelopes spread out on the table in Jake's room. Cat shuffled through some of them. "These look like titles and deeds." She picked up a square envelope. There was something hard inside. She pulled out two photographic plates. "What's this, I wonder?"

Jake fished out something wrapped in tissue paper. "These must be the photographs."

They studied the two pictures of a dammed stream. At the bottom of a hill, a fork went one way and a wood structure channeled most of the water the other. Cat shook her head. "I don't understand."

Jake scowled. "I think I do. I just need proof, but I think this is what your father is after." He pointed at the stream. "I think that's Sugar Springs."

A barrage of emotions engulfed Cat. "You mean he *was* diverting the water?"

"This small fork is going toward Callahan's ranch. By diverting most of the water the other way, he could enrich his largest pasture. It also is going toward the Henderson spread." He paused a moment. "The pieces are falling into place. Henderson was extorting a hundred dollars a month from your father with these photographs."

Cat felt physically sick. "But you'd think that Henderson being killed would get Father off the hook." Then the thought hit her. "Did my father put Ned Hadley up to killing Henderson?" She looked at Jake in shock. "And to kill you, too?" She dissolved into tears. Jake rose and drew her up into an embrace, soothing her.

Jake pulled back and opened his mouth, then hesitated. "Maybe we should turn this information over to the sheriff."

Cat couldn't breathe for a moment. "Turn my father in? I just can't!"

He grasped her shoulders. "Cat, he committed murder."

"Couldn't that be justifiable homicide, since Henderson was blackmailing him?"

"What about Hadley?"

"Ned?"

"Didn't you see your father ride out of town the night he was poisoned?"

Cat was beside herself. She was teetering on the brink of hysteria. "What have I done?" she cried out.

Jake held her tight. "It's not your fault. Albert probably would have found a way to get out from under Henderson's blackmail somehow."

Cat pulled away and sat in the chair again, beating her fists on her forehead. "I should be the loyal daughter and give the plates and photographs to him."

"Yes. But Albert knows we would eventually figure out what happened. I think he poisoned Hadley because it all would have come out in the trial. Murder is much worse than diverting water. What do you think he'd do to silence us?" He put his hand on her shoulder. "Think, Catherine."

She rested her head on her arms. "I don't know what to think or do anymore."

He gently urged her to her feet. "Come, Cat. We have to do the right thing and end the killing right here, before more people get hurt. We have to take the evidence to the sheriff and let him decide what to do."

Like a mindless rag doll, she watched as he put the damning items into one of the envelopes and put the rest of the papers in a drawer of his desk. "I'll keep the rest of the papers here for now." They went through the back streets to the sheriff's office.

The sheriff glanced up as they came in. "Afternoon, Mr. Spencer, Miss Monroe. What can I do for you?"

Jake handed him the envelope and told him where they'd found the contents. The sheriff digested the story and evidence carefully.

The sheriff glanced at Cat. "You know what this means for your father, if this is all true?"

She slowly agreed, wishing a giant hole would appear in the floor and swallow her up. "I want it all to stop."

The sheriff stood and waved to a deputy. "Asa, you're coming with me to Sugar Springs. We're going to arrest Albert Monroe for murder."

Cat shuddered, but said, "I want to go with you."

The sheriff looked back at her from the door. "I don't think that's a good idea."

"Sheriff, I have to face up to him."

Jake grabbed her arm. "We'll both go." They hurried back to their horses and met the sheriff and Asa in front of the sheriff's office. The sheriff handed him a badge.

"I'll have to swear you in as a deputy."

Jake nodded and solemnly swore. The pair mounted up, and they all rode out of town. The dry breeze swirled up the dust in little eddies around them. Looking down, Cat watched the rocks and tufts of grass pass by. She felt like the worst kind of traitor. What loyal family member would do this? Suddenly Jake cleared his throat.

"You're beating yourself down again, aren't you?"

The tears burned trails down her cheeks, and she dashed them away. "This is the worst thing I've ever had to do."

Jake shook his head. "Remember this was your father's doing, not yours."

The group turned a bend in the road and saw two men riding toward them. Cat gasped. "That's Father and

Karl!"

Jake pointed to a copse of trees by the road. "Get off your horse and stay over there."

Cat dismounted and led Sage behind a tree trunk. The three men waited until her father was in shouting distance.

The sheriff moved his horse forward. "Albert Monroe! I want to talk to you!"

Her father pulled up in front of the sheriff. "What do you want?"

"Hand me your pistol. I'm putting you under arrest for the murder of Ned Hadley and the planning of the murder of Logan Henderson."

A dark expression came over Albert Monroe's face. "What proof do you have?"

"We know Henderson was extorting money from you. That was a perfect reason to kill him. Also, you were seen leaving town the night Hadley was killed."

"Who—?" Then he spotted Cat by the tree. "You?"

Cat's hands tightened around the reins. A small noise rose from her throat.

"Damn you, girl! You found the photographs, didn't you?" He dismounted and took a few steps toward her.

Cat's fingers crawled to her neck. "Yes, I did," she squeaked.

"How could you? Why didn't you come to me with them?"

Then she remembered. "Because you were trying to marry me off to a man who was planning to poison me. Yes, Father. That's how Henderson's first wife died!"

That stunned him enough that he didn't see the

sheriff get off his horse and remove Albert's gun. The sheriff waved his own gun. "Get on your horse. We're going into town."

When both were once again mounted, the sheriff clamped handcuffs on Albert's wrists. Through gritted teeth, Albert said, "Karl, go home and tell John."

His foreman hesitated. "Yes, sir." He turned his horse and started back.

The sheriff glanced at Jake. "Coming?"

Jake removed the badge and gave it to the sheriff. "I'm going to escort Miss Monroe home."

The sheriff nodded and turned his horse toward town. Jake dismounted and held Cat. She snuggled into his protective arms. "How did you know I wanted to go home?"

He pulled back. "I've come to know you very well." He kissed her on the forehead. "Let's go."

Without a word, she mounted her horse, and they rode to her inherited home. She should have felt relief to have the mystery solved, but the shadow of gloom over her grew larger by the minute.

Chapter 20

Jake tied the horses at the trough and watched Cat slowly climb the porch steps. A rocking chair near the wall moved in the breeze, and she sat and put her face in her hands. His heart went out to her. In a few strides, he was on the porch beside her. He leaned against the railing and put his hand on her shoulder. "Cat, I'm sorry you had to go through that."

She pulled a handkerchief out of her reticule and dried her tears. "I keep asking myself if things would have been different if I never came here. I think this is all my fault."

He grasped her arms. "Look at me. Henderson was blackmailing him long before you got here. I'm sure your father would have put a stop to it one way or the other. He just made the wrong decision."

The pounding of horse's hooves made them both glance up. John Monroe came riding up the drive. He spurred his steed next to the porch. "Woman, what have you done?"

Cat sobbed out. "John, I—"

"You've put Pa away for murder!" he interrupted. "I don't want to see hide nor hair of you on Sugar Springs. If you do, I'll shoot to kill. And that means you, too, Spencer. I'd bet everything you put her up to this."

Jake balled his fist. "You bullheaded idiot! Don't

you see your pa brought this on himself? Now leave your sister alone!"

John wheeled his horse around. "She's no sister of mine! She wouldn't do this to family. Go to hell, the both of you!" His horse galloped away, raising a cloud of dust behind.

Cat hunched down in the chair, sobbing as if her heart was broken. Jake pulled her up and held her tight as her storm of tears gradually wore itself out. Then he walked her to the door, where Bill waited. Bill waved his hand toward the housekeeper, standing by the stairs. "Let May take Miss Monroe to her room. She has laudanum to help her sleep."

Jake hesitated. "Maybe I should go with her."

Bill inclined his head. "Mr. Spencer, we've grown to respect Miss Monroe. Be assured that no harm will come to her."

Jake felt that Bill was genuine and he could leave her there safely, so he tipped his hat. "Thank you." He kissed Cat's forehead. "I'll be back, sweetheart."

She had ceased sobbing, but was almost catatonic as May led her upstairs. Jake felt a boulder in the pit of his stomach. "Bill, have someone with her every second. Don't let her be alone."

Bill nodded. "I understand, sir."

Jake gave Cat's horse to Toby to bed down, then took off into town. He had business to do. As he was riding, he jotted down notes in his notebook. He stopped at the newspaper office and tossed the paper onto Harvey's desk. "Here's what went on this afternoon. You can write it up as you like."

Harvey took a look, and his mouth gaped. "Jumpin' Jehoshaphat! Are you sure about this?"

"I was there. I have some business to do." Jake mounted his horse and went to the sheriff's office. He swung off and strode into the door.

The sheriff glanced up from his desk. "Spencer! What do you want?"

Jake stood in front of him. "I want to talk to Albert Monroe."

The sheriff appraised him. "Do you think that's a good idea?"

"There are things he needs to know."

The sheriff shrugged and waved his hand toward the back room. "Help yourself."

Albert was reclined on the bunk with his feet resting against the stone wall. Jake stopped by the locked cell door. "Albert, I want to talk to you."

Albert turned his angry face toward him. "I have nothing to say to you, boy."

Jake leaned against the bars. "You don't have to say anything. I want you to listen."

"I don't have to listen to you."

"I'm going to talk anyway, and you can't go anywhere. You have a daughter who's in dark melancholy because of you."

Albert snorted. "I have no daughter."

Jake continued, "Do you know what she went through to try to find you? She spent several months going from town to town, looking through tax rolls, checking on any Monroes she found. When she found you in Tombstone, you rejected her. Yes, I know you thought she was dead, but you didn't give her a chance. Almost immediately you tried to marry her off to a man who had slowly poisoned his first wife to death. What kind of deal did you cut with Henderson? And did you care that you were putting her in danger?"

Albert dropped his feet to the floor. "Who are you to talk to me this way?"

"Someone who loves her and is scared she will take her own life because of you."

Albert was silent for a few moments. "What do you want from me?"

"I want you to tell her that this isn't her fault. That you were responsible for your own dastardly deeds. You don't realize how overjoyed she was when she found you. Don't ruin her life any more than you already have."

Albert watched the toe of his boot. "Bring her to me tomorrow." Then he lay back on the bunk again.

Jake figured that was a dismissal, so he turned. "I'll be in with her tomorrow morning." He nodded to the sheriff as he left.

Jake left his horse at the livery stable and pulled himself up the steps to his room. He removed his outer clothing and poured some water into the basin on the washstand. The cool water felt so good against his face and neck. He toweled down and glanced at his reflection in the mirror. *Do I look that old?* His face stared at him with deep circles under his eyes.

Opening the cabinet door, he extracted a whiskey bottle kept for medicine, poured some of the amber liquid into one of the cups, and downed it in one gulp. He climbed into bed to try to get some sleep, and failed.

****

Cat woke with the morning sun peeking through the open window. The fresh cool air played around her face. She stretched and sat up, then leaned back again when the dizziness hit her. A soft snoring made her look around in surprise to find May sleeping on the chaise. *But why is she here?* Then the fog began to clear, and she remembered yesterday. A deep sadness enveloped her.

May stirred and opened her eyes. She came over to the side of the bed. "Are you awake, Miss Monroe?"

As an answer, Cat pulled the covers up to her chin, and tears rolled down her cheeks. "Leave me," came out, barely audible.

May went to the bell cord and pulled it. "I'm going to have breakfast brought up."

"I'm not hungry. Go."

A knock came to the door, and May let the maid in with a breakfast tray. May directed her to put it on the bedstand beside Cat. "Now here it will sit until you eat something. Miss Monroe, you'll not be good for anything if you let yourself get sick."

"She's right," came a male voice from the hall. "You eat and get dressed. We have an errand to run today."

"Jake," Cat said with a mixture of horror and relief. "I don't want to see anyone or go anywhere."

He strode in past the housekeeper and the maid. He pointed to the tray. "Eat. You need the strength. You didn't eat supper last night. I'll give you a half hour. If you're not down by then, I'm coming up to get you." He turned and left the room.

Cat hesitated. She took a bowl of compote off the tray and downed a couple of spoonfuls while the women waited. Her stomach twisted as much from hunger as from tension. Some tea and toast was all the more she could manage. "That's all I can eat."

The maid left with the tray, and May gave a slight

incline of her head. "I'll help you get dressed. Mr. Spencer arrived in a carriage, so I'll get out a day dress for you."

Emotions left Cat. She merely helped while May fixed her hair and fastened her clothing, and she walked downstairs with a sensation of not being in her body but watching herself from afar. Mechanically she put on her gloves, picked up her reticule, and pulled her parasol from the stand.

Jake, with a worried glance, walked her outside and helped her into the carriage. When he hopped onto the driver's seat, he took her hand and squeezed it. "I'll be with you, if you need me today." He kissed her hand and gathered the reins. Giving them a snap, he guided the horses to the road.

She was aware of the smell of new-mown hay from the field across the road. The cool morning breeze played around her face as she opened the parasol to shield her from the harsh sunrays. Their time on the road was spent in silence except for the clopping of the horse's hooves and the rattling of the carriage wheels. It was not until they pulled up in front of the sheriff's office that she spoke. "Oh, no, Jake, I can't."

He squeezed her hand again. "I had a talk with your father last night. He wants to see you." He helped her down, and they walked into the office. The sheriff glanced up and nodded before he took the ring of keys and led them into the back room. Her father was standing stoically by the barred window in his cell. The key released the bolt with a clang. The sheriff waved his hand. "You may go in, Miss Monroe."

She went in with her hand clamped around Jake's arm. He patted her hand. "I'll leave you here to talk. I'll be outside, if you need me."

She released him, the sheriff closed and locked the metal door again, and he and Jake left them alone.

Albert cleared his throat. "Catherine, sit." He indicated the bunk. She obeyed. "Since things look bad for me, I may as well take young Spencer's advice and unburden myself."

"I'm sorry, Father," she said barely audible.

He crossed to her and cupped her chin. "Look at me, Cat. You have nothing to apologize for. I, on the other hand, have used you terribly. Just listen." He leaned against the wall. "I've done a number of things in my life which I've regretted. But I hate myself for the way I used you."

"Used me?"

"I know I accused Jake of using you for that newspaper story. That doesn't hold a candle to what I've done. After the initial shock of finding out you were really my daughter— Well, I should start this from the beginning." He sat next to her. "Yes, those pictures are of Sugar Springs. When I purchased the land, the larger fork was toward Callahan's ranch. The best pasture on my acreage was in the other direction, so I channeled the water toward that, leaving enough to go to the Callahan pasture. I was hoping it wouldn't raise suspicion. It also benefited the neighboring pasture.

"Logan Henderson acquired that land a few years later. His wife was sickly and died a short time later. Believe me, I didn't know he killed her. One evening, he came over and showed me he had photographic evidence that I was diverting the water, but he said he would keep silent if I paid him a hundred dollars a month. I had substantial reserves, but it hurt to pay him twelve hundred a year, so I was looking for a way out. Then you came to town." He took a breath like he was gathering his thoughts.

Cat watched him closely. "You did make a deal with him, didn't you?"

He put his hand gently on hers. "He came to me soon after you arrived and said he would destroy the photographs and plates if I would give him your hand in marriage, but there was something else he wanted. He wanted me to change my will so he would get half of my south pasture, which is in line with his property. I told him I would only agree to that if he would leave me his pasture in his will. I was hoping you would accept his proposal, but as time went on, it looked like you wouldn't. Logan told me he was going to call Spencer out the night of the masquerade."

"So that's when you decided to kill him. Why did you have Ned shoot Jake, too?"

He paused. "Partially, so the boy wouldn't be blamed. Also in hopes he would stay away from you. I figured it was all over when I got his land and cattle and you got the house. Ned was the one who was sure Jake saw him shoot Logan and went on a campaign to get rid of the witness. I didn't know of his plan to kill Jake, too. The burning of the barn was an accident."

"Why did you poison Ned Hadley?"

He blew out a breath slowly. "All the plans were caving in on me. I had to go along with taking Ned into town to be locked up. Then I grew concerned when Ned asked for a lawyer. I knew all the dirty details were going to come out. So I poisoned him before he could spill the truth."

Her heart was breaking. She squeezed his hand. "I

keep blaming myself. If I hadn't come here it never would have happened."

"Catherine, it would have happened one way or the other. I made some foolish decisions and involved you. It's my place to say I'm sorry." He paused. "I don't know what the jury and judge are going to do with my trial, but I had to clear the air with you. I know you can take care of yourself. I'm very proud to call you my daughter." He rose and took her up into an embrace. "Cat, I know your mother would be proud of you, too. You remind me so much of her."

"Thank you, Father." She found comfort in his arms but knew she couldn't stay. "Sheriff, Jake! I'm ready to go." She dabbed her eyes with her handkerchief as the two men entered the room. The sheriff let her out of the cell, and her father extended his hand to Jake. "Spencer, take good care of my little girl."

Jake shook his hand warmly. "You bet I will, sir."

Cat went out on Jake's arm feeling a weight had lifted off her. But the concern she had for her father's trial was still there.

Chapter 21

The morning sun was still a golden glow as Cat, Jake, Toby, and two of the hired men loaded the materials for the barn into the wagons. Cat paid Otto in bank notes the hundred and five dollars she owed, and they assembled the caravan with Cat riding in front and Jake taking the lead wagon.

"Ready?" she called out to the others. At their shouts, she replied, "Let's go!" She was answered with a rattling of harnesses, a clopping of hooves, and a squeaking of wheels. She rode silently by Jake as they wound their way through town. On the outskirts, she said, "I hope we have enough men to be able to raise the barn."

Jake glanced at her. "We have Toby and the five hands. I think that will be enough to at least get the frame up today."

Cat thought it would have been nice to have the Sugar Springs hands to help her, as well, but she hadn't heard from John since he'd berated her. She heard a shout behind and turned around. Three men galloped up on horseback. She recognized her brother Daniel. "Daniel! Is something wrong?"

He rode up beside her. "I saw Pa yesterday, and he said you may need help raising the barn. We're off from the mine for a few days, so I thought you could use the hands. This here's Luke and Will."

She grinned. "Thank you all. Yes, we can use as many as we can get."

The parade arrived at the house and rounded the drive into the back where the barn's cleared foundations lay. Cat and Jake moved one of the garden plank benches over to a spot near the site, and Cat set up the hardware and tools there while the men unloaded the wagons.

Hettie, the cook, came down to speak with Cat, wiping her hands on her apron. "Miss Monroe, I just got a shipment of lemons from California. Would you like for me to make some lemonade for the men?"

"That sounds splendid. I'll come help you." She saw Jake take one of the hammers. "Jake, could you and Toby be the foremen? I'm going to help Hettie in the kitchen."

He kissed her on the forehead. "Of course, darlin'."

Hettie's kitchen always smelled wonderful. Cat knew it was bad taste to have odors from the kitchen in the house, but she never minded it. In fact, she had learned to cook and bake from Gardenia, her aunt's chef, a former slave, and had learned to tell when a dish was done just by the smell.

Hettie set a large stone urn on the oilcloth-covered work table and pulled a large wooden crate from the pantry. A crowbar loosened the top, and the room filled with the sharp citrus smell. Hettie produced two paring knives and juicers.

Cat rolled each fruit on the table, then sliced it in half and squeezed it, being careful to pick the pips out. Hettie gave her an earthenware ewer, and when it was filled with juice, Cat emptied it into the urn. Hettie worked out how many ewers were in the urn, then added water from the cistern pump, which always ran clear and cold. Hettie was just about to add the sugar when Cat heard horses coming into the drive.

Bill appeared at the kitchen door. "Miss Monroe, Mr. Callahan and a few others are here to see you."

Cat dipped her hands into the dry sink basin and wiped them. "I wonder what they want?" She hurried to the porch, where Callahan waited.

He removed his hat. "Miss Monroe, I heard you were going to raise your barn today, and I wanted to help. I know there's been bad blood between your family and me, but now that it's come out in the open, I don't hold it against you." He extended his hand. "Neighbors should help one another."

Cat was stopped with surprise for a moment, but she grasped his calloused hand with her own. "Thank you, Mr. Callahan. I appreciate your help. Jake and my foreman, Toby, are in charge."

He put his hat back on and tipped it to her. "You're welcome, miss." There were several men with him, and Cat wondered if one was Jake's father.

Peggy rode to the house and waved. "Can you use some help here?" She hopped down and tied her horse to the hitching post.

Cat gave her a hug. "I'm so happy to see you! Can you give us a hand in the kitchen?"

They went to the kitchen and found Hettie chipping ice from the icebox into the urn. She put the heavy lid on then, and the girls gathered the ewers and started to fill them. After making a space on the bench that held the hardware, Cat, Peggy, and Hettie set the ewers there with towels over them and some tin cups on the end.

Jake and a few men came over. Jake indicated an

older version of himself. "Cat Monroe, this is my pa, Lincoln Spencer."

Lincoln tipped his hat. "Pleased to meet you, Miss Monroe." He smiled, but she could see suspicion in his eyes.

"Pleased to meet you, too. Have some lemonade? Hettie, Peggy, and I will be making some ham sandwiches and molasses cookies soon, also. All the workers are welcome to eat."

The men partook of the refreshment and went back to work, while the girls returned to the kitchen, where Hettie was slicing two large loaves of bread. The sharp, sweet smell of the baking cookies made Cat's mouth water.

Cat sat at the work table and started assembling sandwiches. She glanced out the window toward Sugar Springs. Yes, she noticed nobody from her family's ranch had come over to help, and it made her very sad. *I may have gained Callahan and Jake's family, but I've lost my own.* The first platter of sandwiches went out to the bench. She gave another look down the road as she covered the food with a towel.

****

Jake removed his hat and wiped his brow with a bandanna. The sun was marking one more half hour in the western sky. The work had been long and hard, but in front of him stood an almost completed barn with the skeleton of a roof in place. He, Toby, and the hired men would assemble that tomorrow.

His pa came over and slapped him on the back. "I'll help you return the wagons to town."

"Thanks." He turned to Toby. "Could you and one of the other men take the other two?"

"Sure." Toby went to the wagons.

Peggy mounted her horse and rode to Jake. "All of you did a good job on the barn. See you around, big brother!" At his grin and wave, she turned her horse toward home.

Soon they were lined up in the drive. Jake climbed the steps to the porch, where Cat watched. "I'm leaving, sweetheart. I'll be back in the morning to help with the roof." He kissed her on her forehead and didn't want to stop there. He'd love to take an excursion around her fascinating curves, but he knew there would be other times. Looking deep into her eyes, he knew she was having the same feelings.

The corners of her lips curled up. "Tomorrow, then."

He tore himself away and hopped into the driver's seat on the lead wagon. "Ready?" At everyone's shout, he snapped the reins of the team, and the caravan headed to town. They made it to the yard before the office closed and each man untied his horse from the back of the wagon he'd driven.

Lincoln rode to Jake. "Son, I'll buy you a drink at the Oriental."

Jake swung up into the saddle and said farewell to Toby, who headed back to the ranch. He urged his horse and caught up to his pa. The twilight was deepening as the dim golden glow of lamplight floated out from the saloon windows. The colors on the glass made strange patterns in the street and walkways. Tinny music was interspersed with loud voices and fists hitting various parts of a body. Jake grimaced. A typical evening in Tombstone.

The cigar-smoke air hit them as they pushed

through the swinging doors. Jake sat at an empty table while Lincoln ordered two mugs of brew and then watched him make his way around the tables and set a cold one in front of Jake. The beer went down real easy after the long day of manual labor.

Lincoln wiped the foam from his mustache and sat back. "Good work today, son. That Monroe girl isn't an ass like her poor excuse of a father. Maybe 'cause she wasn't brought up by him." He paused. "Tell me. Are you inclined to have her?"

Jake stared at his mug. "She's smart for a woman, and she's got gumption. There are few women like her. Yes, I want her."

"She's got money, too. I guess it wouldn't be so bad to be tied in with the Monroes, now that the truth's come out. And she's the one who put the prickly pear in his pants."

Jake frowned. "There's more to this story than meets the eye."

There was a commotion near the entrance, and John Monroe burst in, pointing at Jake. "There you are! Ned shoulda plugged you when he had the chance." He weaved across the room, knocking into chairs and tables. "Someone should tell you to keep your nose outta everybody's business."

Jake stood as John stumbled into him. "You're drunk. Go sleep it off. I'll let that go because you're Cat's brother."

"That traitorous she-wolf is not my sister. She ruined my family." He eyed Jake unsteadily, then took a swing with his fist. "So did you."

Jake caught his wrist and leaned toward his pa. "I'm going to have to do this. Could you find him a room?"

Lincoln nodded and rose. "Yep. Do what you have to."

Jake took a wriggling John outside and aimed a fist square to John's jaw. John went out like a light, right into Lincoln's arms. Jake rubbed his sore hand. "Thanks, Pa."

Lincoln hefted John over his shoulder. "Don't think of it. I'll help you tomorrow on the roof."

Jake put on his hat. "Tomorrow." He headed to his apartment.

Chapter 22

The cool breeze billowed the lace curtains in the parlor. Bill brought in a ewer of lemonade and two glasses. "Anything else before dinner, Miss Monroe?"

Cat glanced up. "No, no, thank you." As Bill left, she turned to Jake. "They scheduled the trial for next week Monday? That's just a few days before Christmas."

Jake poured a glass and handed it to her. "I guess they wanted to get it over with by then." He put his arm around her shoulders as he watched Toby and the hands move the horses into the newly finished barn.

Her relief at having the barn completed in two days was replaced by the gloom of her father's fate. "I'm almost more afraid to see John there than of what will befall father. At least I've made my peace with him."

Jake gave her a squeeze. "John will come around."

She shook her head. "I don't know, after what you told me about last evening." She glanced at the clock. "I should dress for dinner."

Jake shrugged. "It's just us. After a long day, I don't think it matters what we wear at dinner."

She set her glass on the tray. "I want to wash up, though. I'll return in a few minutes." As Cat went upstairs, she noticed Jake went outside toward the pump.

Cat poured the water into the basin on her

washstand and splashed the cool liquid on her face. Taking the towel, she studied her eyes as she dried off. *I look so tired and worn.* She immediately pinched her cheeks to get some color. She picked up the brush at the vanity and smoothed her hair, then took the long, single braid down her back and pinned it up.

From below, she heard Bill. "Miss Monroe! Dinner is served."

"I'll be right down." After a final pinch, she hurried into the dining room, where Jake stood behind her chair.

He pulled it out. "You look wonderful."

"Thank you, sir."

He seated himself across from her. "So do you."

A savory-smelling chicken stew was set before them, and a heaping platter of biscuits. Butter and honey was placed within reach. For a few minutes, they attacked the food with gusto, and then Jake sat back.

"I've decided I'll give you the most festive Christmas you ever had. Just leave it to me."

"You'll be with me at the trial, won't you?"

Jake leaned forward and grasped her hand. "You bet I will. But you need something to make you happy, too."

She digested that and squeezed his hand. "I want to see the wellspring of Sugar Springs. That was the thing that caused all this. I have to convince John to make it right again."

Jake blinked. "You're asking a lot. I don't think you'll be welcomed with open arms over there."

"That's why I'm going alone tomorrow. After what happened with John and you last night, I'll be better off facing them by myself."

Jake pulled a pained expression. "Be careful, and don't make any bullheaded decisions. With any sign of trouble, promise me you'll turn and walk away."

"Jake—"

"Promise me." There was steel in his eyes.

She bit her lip. "All right. I promise." He didn't realize she had a king's ex behind her back.

****

Cat pulled up Sage at the gate of Sugar Springs ranch. It seemed so long since she'd first arrived and found her family.

A cloud of gloom settled in. How could she have known what havoc would come of it? She turned her horse into the drive and started toward the house.

Halfway there, she saw dust rising behind the hill and heard hoofbeats pounding. A figure rode to meet her.

She shielded her eyes against the morning sun and recognized Karl. Stopping her horse, she waited for him.

He tipped his hat. "Miss Cat? I come to tell you you're not wanted here."

Cat thought fast. "Karl, I've come to visit Mrs. Monroe. Please escort me to the cabin."

"I c-can't. It's against orders."

Cat opened her reticule and pointed her gun at him. "I'd hate to shoot you, but I will if you don't do as I ask." She put out her hand. "Let me have your gun." He hesitated. "I do know how to use this. Your gun, please." Slowly, he removed it from the holster. She smiled as she waved her gun. "Now ride ahead of me."

It was a solemn small parade that made it to the path to the cabin. When Cat saw Polly hanging out clothes on the line, she took Karl's gun and tossed it into the bushes on the other side of the path.

While Karl got down to look for it, Cat turned her horse toward the cabin.

Sam and Aggie greeted her in the yard. "Auntie Cat! Look Ma, it's Auntie Cat!"

Polly hurried over. "Children, go inside and fill the buckets with fresh water for me."

They turned and ran for the door. "Yes, Ma!"

Cat hopped down, and the two women embraced each other. Polly pulled back. "You shouldn't have come here."

Cat heard Karl going through the bushes looking for his gun. "I had to. I must see the spring that caused all this trouble."

Polly shook her head. "John is out checking on the stock. He'll see you, and there will be trouble, for sure." Her voice lowered. "I have been working on a plan to get you two together again, but you must do as I say. Please, go back to your house until after the trial."

Cat frowned. "Could you let me in on it?"

Polly grasped her arm. "There's not enough time now. You have to trust me."

Cat felt put out, but she was willing to try anything. "I will."

Polly gave her arm a squeeze. "Now, go. Karl is coming down the path."

She remounted her horse just as Karl reached them with his gun trained on her. "Leave the ranch now!" he growled.

She turned and spurred her horse to the drive. "I'm going."

Cat heard Polly say, "Please don't tell John Miss

Monroe was here, Karl, for my sake."

She was too far away to hear his reply, but she hoped Polly knew John well enough to be able to fix this.

Chapter 23

Cat waited as Jake climbed down from the carriage and came around to give her a hand to the walk. The gleaming courthouse seemed foreboding compared to the time, months ago, when she was searching for her father and had viewed it with high hopes. She gave a shaky sigh. "This is one of the worst days of my life."

Jake offered his arm. "I'll be right beside you the whole time."

She slipped her hand through. "I am grateful."

The whitewashed courtroom was ablaze in light from the large side windows. Polished mahogany risers for the judge's desk and the witness stand echoed the fence and gate that separated the players from the audience. Jake guided Cat to a couple of empty chairs behind the defendant's table near the outside wall.

The county prosecutor, Ezra Tanner, was already in his chair, looking stone-faced and ready for war. He had a stack of crisp papers and other items on the table in front of him. Cat recognized the photographic plates off to one side.

Jake had his notebook out and was jotting. Before she could ask a question, he said, "I promised Harvey, since I was going to be here, I'd get the story."

She sighed, resigned that he would always be a newspaperman, no matter what. And, unfortunately, this was big news in the town.

People were filing in, settling in the available chairs. Ed and Edna came over and sat beside them. Edna leaned over and patted Cat's shoulder. "We're here to support you in any way we can."

Cat put her hand on Edna's. "Thank you so much. I've missed being able to talk to you."

"You're welcome to our house anytime."

Cat smiled. "And you to mine."

A murmur went through the assemblage, and Cat turned to see Daniel come in with Dara on his arm. How bold he is to bring a Bird Cage girl in here, Cat thought. Even though Cat knew Dara's story, she understood the reaction.

Callahan and Lincoln Spencer arrived and sat in the back. They were followed by John and Polly, who sat directly behind the defendant's table. John didn't look at them, but Polly nodded in Cat's direction.

The bailiff opened the windows, and a cool morning breeze fanned around the ostrich feather in Cat's hat. The room was getting stuffy with all the warm bodies in it, and she was glad she and Jake had chosen seats where they were.

Her heart dropped when the sheriff came in with her father in shackles. His lawyer, Mr. Worthy, sat beside him at the table, and the sheriff took a chair to one side.

The twelve men of the jury filed in and took their seats in the box by the far wall. Cat searched their faces, hoping for a friendly one, but they all looked stern and solemn.

The bailiff came forward. "All rise. The Right Honorable Judge Loyal Gibson has entered court." The judge in his robes climbed the wooden steps to his boxed throne and brought the court to order. Everyone sat at his request. He picked up some papers off his desk.

"We've assembled here for the trial of Albert Monroe, who has been accused of arranging the murder of Logan Henderson and the attempted murder of Jake Spencer. Also, for the willful murder of Ned Hadley. What say you? Guilty or not guilty?"

Worthy stood. "Not guilty, your honor."

The judge turned to the prosecutor. "You may give your opening statement, Mr. Tanner."

Cat listened to Tanner with a lump in her throat. *Why, oh, why, has it come to this? I know I'm not responsible, but I keep feeling like this all happened because I came here.* As if knowing what she was thinking, Jake took her hand and squeezed it. She glanced at him through the tears that burned her eyes.

The prosecutor called John Monroe to the stand. John swore on the Bible to tell the truth and then seated himself in the witness box.

Tanner leaned against the prosecutor's table. "Mr. Monroe, can you give the events leading up to the crime? Were you privy to the details?"

John fingered his hat on his lap. "Yes, sir, I was." He paused. "It started when Logan Henderson found out we were diverting water from the spring to our larger southern pasture. He hired a photographer to take a picture of the spring and the wooden-wall dam we put up. Most of the natural bed for the water went west through the Callahan ranch. Our western pasture was small, so we fed the fork that went through the southern pasture. That went toward the Henderson ranch, also."

Tanner picked up the two photographic plates and

the pictures. "This is exhibit numbers one through four." He handed John the items. "Are these the photographs of the diverted spring?"

"Yes, they are." John gave them back to Tanner.

"What was the purpose of taking the photographs?"

"Mr. Henderson threatened to expose the diversion if we didn't give him payment of one hundred dollars a month."

"Why would he do that, if it was benefiting him to have more water in his pasture?"

John leaned forward. "Because he wanted half of our southern pasture that adjoined his property, and Pa wouldn't sell it to him."

"Is that what led to Mr. Henderson's murder?"

"Partly. A deal to get out from under it went bad."

"What deal was that?"

John nodded toward Cat. "When my sister, Catherine Monroe, showed up, Henderson came to us with a deal. He could marry Catherine and our families would be joined. Each would make out a new will. If Pa went first, Henderson would get half of the southern pasture. If Henderson went first, Pa would get all of his pasture land and cattle. Catherine would get the house and yard. If that was agreed on, Pa didn't have to pay any more and the photographs and plates would be destroyed."

"How did the deal go bad?"

"Catherine didn't want anything to do with Logan. Pa and Logan finally went to the church and tried to arrange a wedding. Catherine kept resisting. Then Logan was shot by Ned Hadley."

"Did your father have any knowledge of what Ned Hadley was going to do?"

John paused. "I don't know."

"You weren't privy to any discussions between your father and Hadley about Henderson?"

"No, sir."

Tanner sat on a chair. "I'm finished with this witness."

The judge turned to the defense. "Mr. Worthy, do you have any questions for this witness?"

"No questions."

The judge nodded to John. "You may step down. Next witness?"

Tanner removed another sheet of paper. "Your honor, I call Jake Spencer to the stand."

Jake gave Cat's hand a squeeze and rose, making his way to the front. He was sworn in and seated himself in the witness box.

Tanner moved to stand in front of Jake. "Mr. Spencer, could you relate to us what happened between you and Mr. Henderson the night of the masquerade ball."

"Catherine, my sister Peggy, and I were talking when Henderson came to our table and grabbed Catherine by the hair and told me he didn't want me seeing her. We got into a fight and then were told by the sheriff to take it outside or he was going to arrest both of us. Henderson went out ahead of me, and I stopped and strapped on my gun because I didn't trust him. He called to me outside, and then there were shots fired from the corner of the building."

"Did you see who fired at you?"

"No. I was hit in the shoulder and went down. That's when people started to come out."

"You and Miss Monroe were the ones who exposed

the deal of Henderson's extortion of Albert Monroe, am I right?"

"Yes, but that was after he was killed."

"The night Ned Hadley was poisoned, you witnessed Albert Monroe in Tombstone, did you not?"

"Catherine and I were at Trail's Restaurant and saw Mr. Monroe riding out."

Tanner sat down. "No more questions for this witness."

The judge turned to Worthy. "Your witness."

Worthy stood. "Mr. Spencer, you and Mr. Henderson were rivals for the hand of Miss Monroe?"

Jake hesitated. "In a way. Albert wanted her to marry Henderson, but she didn't want to."

"So it would be better for both of you if Mr. Henderson was out of the picture."

Tanner stood. "Your honor, I object!"

The judge turned to Worthy. "Really, Mr. Worthy, is this statement necessary?"

Worthy spread his hands in front of him. "Your honor, I was just trying to show that others had reason and motive to kill Logan Henderson."

The judge paused. "I'll tolerate this for now, but you'd better have some kind of proof behind it."

Worthy stood in front of Jake. "Mr. Spencer, did you engage Mr. Hadley to kill Logan Henderson?" Cat gave an audible intake of breath.

Jake's mouth was in a straight line. "No, I did not. Why would I have him shoot me, too?"

"Maybe to divert attention from yourself. Or Miss Monroe."

Jake put his fist to the railing. "Neither one of us plotted to kill Henderson *or* engaged Ned Hadley to shoot him."

The judge glared at Worthy. "Without any proof, I think you should drop this line of questioning."

Worthy set down his papers on the table. "No further questions."

As Jake left the stand, Tanner called his next witness. "Miss Catherine Monroe."

Jake gripped her shoulders when he passed her. Cat appreciated that, but her stomach was all in knots. She swore on the Bible and took the stand, hoping she looked calmer than she felt.

Tanner stood in front of her. "Tell me, Miss Monroe, where were you when you heard the gunshots at the masquerade?"

"I was around the corner of the building, in the carriage yard."

"Was anyone with you?"

"My family—Polly, John, and my father."

"What did you do when you heard the shots?"

"We all ran around the corner to see what had happened."

"Now, this is a very important question, Miss Monroe: What did you see when you got to the scene of the shooting?"

She closed her eyes, and her chest heaved, recalling those horrible moments. "Jake was on the ground, bleeding, and Logan Henderson was lying across the drive from him. I heard hoofbeats on the road and saw a figure, on a brown horse with a white tail, heading out of town."

"Did you know who it was?"

"No. I didn't see his face."

"How did you later know who it was?"

"It was after I received the Henderson house and yard, and Ned Hadley tried to kill us in the barn there. We took off after him, and I realized it was his brown horse with the white tail that I had seen at the masquerade after the shooting."

"Did you also witness your father being in town the night Ned Hadley was poisoned?"

Tears burned her eyes. "Yes, sir."

"No more questions."

The judge nodded at Worthy. "Your witness."

Worthy glanced at Albert, then stood. "Miss Monroe, you received a sizable inheritance from Logan Henderson's will, did you not?"

She felt the blood drain from her face. "Yes, I did."

"And he was under the impression that he was to be married to you, wasn't he?"

"I never agreed to marry him."

"So if Henderson died after the will was drafted, it was to your benefit that he happened to die in a shooting. It would be so easy to arrange it with Ned Hadley yourself, wouldn't it?"

"No! I—" Cat, stunned, stared at him with tears streaming down her face.

In the next few seconds, Tanner rose from his chair with, "I object! He's badgering the witness!"

At the same time Jake jumped up and shouted, "Stop this!"

The judge smashed his gavel down. "Order in the court! Or I'll have everyone removed!" He turned to Worthy. "I have to agree with Mr. Tanner. Miss Monroe isn't on trial here."

Worthy shifted his feet. "I'm just trying to show that Mr. Spencer and Miss Monroe had a reason to see

Logan Henderson dead."

Albert rose from his seat. "Your honor, I want to confess and throw myself on the mercy of the court."

Worthy sputtered. "Albert, you can't!"

The judge banged his gavel down again. "Mr. Monroe, are you sure you want to do this?"

Albert paused. "My daughter spent a number of months trying to find me. I can't sit here and see her blamed for my sins."

"It's up to you if you want to take the stand."

"I do, your honor."

The judge waved his hand. "The witness is excused. Mr. Spencer, could you escort her to her seat?"

Jake strode to the stand and gently grasped Cat by her arm. "Come with me."

Cat rose and silently let him guide her through the gate. When she was seated, Jake clasped her hand in his. She held onto him like she would never let go.

The judge indicated the stand. "Swear the defendant in."

Cat listened as her father confessed to the same things he had told her. John shifted and fidgeted in his chair as he heard what his father had to say.

Albert drew a breath at the end of his speech. "Lastly, I want to make a public apology to my daughter. All I could think of was to use her to get out of my troubles. Catherine, I'm very sorry, and I hope someday you can forgive me."

The silence in the courtroom covered everyone in a stifling cloud. Cat was exhausted, as if she had been traveling for days. Jake put a protective arm around her.

Whispers and murmurs traveled around the jury box. One of them said to the judge, "Your honor, I don't think we need to vote."

The judge broke the tension. "Well. Gentlemen of the jury, what say you?"

The man at the fore stood and glanced at his peers, who all nodded. "In light of the confession, we have no choice but to find Albert Monroe guilty."

The judge banged down his gavel. "The defendant may step down and take your seat." As Albert did so, the judge stood. "I'm calling an hour recess to decide on a sentence. May I see the district attorney and Mr. Worthy in my chambers?"

The sheriff escorted Albert to the door of the courtroom, and Cat caught up with them. She put her hand on his shoulder. "Father, I'm—"

Albert paused and stroked her fingers. "No need to talk. I did what I had to do as a father. Go with Jake."

He glanced at Jake, who was standing behind Cat. "I have a remarkable daughter."

Jake grasped both her shoulders. "You sure do, sir."

The sheriff cleared his throat, and Albert went with him to the jail. Cat leaned against Jake, who nodded toward the street. "Let's go to the ice cream parlor for a phosphate."

She opened her parasol and took his arm. "I don't really want anything, but it will make the time go faster."

****

Jake studied Cat as she occasionally took a sip of the cherry phosphate through her paper straw. She was quieter than usual, and that bothered him. She'd probably had more troubles thrust on her in the last four months than she had experienced most of her life to that point. He deeply wished he could shield her from this and give her nothing but sunshine to replace it, but he knew she had to make it out to the other side of the tunnel. He would be waiting with his arms outstretched to make the melancholy go away.

He looked at his half-drunk root beer and pushed it away. "We should be getting back." He rose from the chair at the small round table and held out his hand.

She gave him a small smile and stood, grasping his fingers with her own. "I was just thinking of all the places I wanted to be instead of here."

He put his hat on and slipped her arm through his. "Me, too."

The stagecoach clattered to a stop as they walked out. A short woman waited with a traveling bag and a trunk the driver hoisted onto the top of the coach. Jake squinted. *I know that woman!* "Dara! Where are you going? I saw you in court this morning with Daniel."

She gazed at him with sad eyes, her face scrubbed of all the paint. She wore a demure traveling dress and hat in place of the flamboyant clothes he was used to seeing on her. "I was biding time until the stage came. I'm going home to Texas to become a respectable citizen again."

"I'm sorry to hear that."

A sharp laugh exploded from her. "What? That I'm going to be respectable?" She glanced at Cat. "You won't miss me. Besides, I got what I came for, and I can lay to rest my family's concern for my sister."

He paused a moment. "I'll be losing my best news source."

She chuckled and gave him a peck on the cheek. "I'm sure you'll find another. Not many people in this town know enough to keep their mouths shut." To Cat, she added, "Don't be jealous, honey. He's all yours."

Jake helped her into the coach. "Farewell, Dara. I'll miss you."

She smirked. "You're one of a kind, handsome. Goodbye!" She waved out the window as the driver snapped the reins.

The dust reached them from the departing coach even though they had stepped up on the walkway.

As the courthouse loomed, Jake felt Cat tremble, and her hand gripped his arm. Her jaw was clenched, but a look of determination steeled her eyes. *The girl has grit.*

People were filing in and taking their seats. Cat glanced toward Polly. Cat must have silently said something to her, because Polly mouthed back, "Not yet."

Jake guided her to the seats behind the defendant's table and waited for Albert's fate. Soon everyone was assembled, and the judge and lawyers returned from the chambers. The audience rose at the words of the bailiff. The judge asked everyone to be seated.

The judge looked at Albert. "Will the defendant please rise?" At the request, Albert did. "You have been found guilty of arranging the murder of Logan Henderson, arranging the attempted murder of Jake Spencer, and the willful murder of Ned Hadley. Usually, that would be enough to hang you. But in light of your complete confession and that you have always been a contributing member of this community and never been outside of the law before, I sentence you to forty years in the territorial penitentiary."

Cat slumped in her chair, and as a murmur went through the court, she said to Jake, "At least he gets to live."

The judge banged his gavel. "Order!" He turned back to Albert, who stood stoically. "You shall be transported by stagecoach with a deputy tomorrow at one o'clock to start your sentence. Do you have anything to say to the court?"

Albert shook his head. "No, your honor."

With a hit of the gavel, the judge pronounced, "Case is closed."

John smashed his hat on his head and, with a murderous glare at Cat and Jake, stalked out with Polly. Cat pursed her lips and rose with Jake. She sighed.

"Let's go home." She wrapped her hand around his arm, and they went to the carriage.

Chapter 24

The late December midday sun was just past its southern zenith as Cat rode into Tombstone. The rays warmed her, but there was a chill in the air. She clasped her cape closer around her chin. Jake was going to meet her at the sheriff's office to see her father off. Her stomach twisted as she recognized John's carriage outside the office. Jake rose from the sidewalk bench in front. She dismounted and tied the reins over the post, and Sage drank gratefully from the trough.

Jake pushed his hat back with his thumb as she stepped up from the street. "John, Polly, and Daniel are in there right now."

She checked her watch brooch. "It's fifteen minutes before he has to leave." As if on cue, the stagecoach rattled in. She blew a nervous breath. "I'm going in."

Jake held the door for her, and she entered to a flurry of activity. Her father appeared with a deputy. Albert's hands and feet were in shackles with chains long enough that he could move but not run.

With a cry, she went to embrace her father when she felt a rough grab on her shoulder and was pulled back. She turned to see John as he whipped her around into the wall. Polly gasped. Daniel and Jake yanked him off. Jake had a fist ready when the sheriff stopped his arm.

"That's enough!" the sheriff barked. "I'm not one to get in the middle of a family hoo-haa, but I won't have it in my office."

"John," Albert said in a weary voice, "I'm not going to the penitentiary with this on my mind. Your sister is the one who deserves an apology from you. I used her to try to get out of the blackmail. It's not her fault I'm in this mess."

John stalked to the outside door and jammed on his hat. "That woman and Spencer can go to blazes as far as I'm concerned. Polly!"

Polly's face was flushed. She grabbed Cat's hand and squeezed it.

John took Polly's arm. "Now! Let's go!" When they were out, he slammed the door behind him.

Albert shook his head. "I hope he comes around." He turned to Daniel. "Are you sure you don't want part of the ranch?"

Daniel shifted his hat around the brim and shuffled his feet. "No, sir. I wasn't cut out to be a cowboy. I'd rather work in town. I've cleaned up, the last few weeks, and was named foreman at the mine."

Albert shook Daniel's hand. "I'm sorry for the things I've said to you in the past. You've grown a lot."

Daniel half smiled. "That means a lot to me, Pa."

Albert kissed Cat on the cheek. "Catherine, I'm proud of the woman you've become. Write to me?"

She kissed him back. "I sure will."

He shook Jake's hand, and the sheriff tapped his shoulder. "Time to go, Albert."

Cat's stomach knotted for her father as he was helped into the coach by the deputy and the sheriff. Such a man like her father shouldn't be chained like an animal. She shuddered. *On the other hand, it's better than swinging from a rope.* With a shout from the driver, the stagecoach rattled down the road and out of her sight.

Jake put his arm around her. "Let's go back to your house. I have a surprise for you."

They waved goodbye to Daniel and climbed onto their horses. The sun had warmed the desert area from the chilly December morning, but the breeze that hit her face was still cold, although not as cold as it would have been in Virginia at that time of year. She was starting to appreciate the more temperate weather in the territory, but she knew she would miss the snow.

Once they had turned into the drive to the house and dismounted, Jake led the animals to the trough and tied the reins. "I'll put Sage in the barn in a few minutes."

Bill met them on the porch. "I did what you requested, Mr. Spencer." He smiled.

Jake nodded. "Thank you, Bill." He turned to Cat. "Close your eyes."

She was completely puzzled but did what she was told. Jake took her hand and led her into the house, where her nose was met with the sharp smell of evergreen. "Oh," escaped her lips.

"Open your eyes."

Cat sucked in a breath. There were fresh evergreen boughs tied with red ribbons in various places around the parlor, including over the hearth. On one of the tables was a small tree with popcorn strings, gaily colored glass ornaments, affixed candles on the ends of the branches, silver tinsel strands, and a white tin star at the top.

She was at a loss for words. Finally, she choked out, "It's beautiful! Did you arrange for this?"

The corners of his lips curled up. "I purchased a lot of the things and sent them to Bill to fix up with the staff."

"Wherever did you find evergreen?"

"It was shipped from the mountains."

On the calling card table she spotted a wreath with red ribbon intertwined with the evergreens. Cat clapped her hands like a child. "Is that for the door?"

Jake picked it up, and they went to the front door, where a nail already had been driven above the leaded glass window. He hung the wreath on it. "Yep. Hope you like my surprise."

Overwhelmed, she burst into tears. "With all the pain...of the last few weeks...I don't deserve...this." She buried her face on his shoulder.

Jake hugged her tight. "Whoa, Nelly, here. Yes, you deserve it. I mean to make your life as happy as I can." He pulled back and made her look at him. "We're going to the reverend and plan a wedding in a couple of weeks." He dried her eyes with his handkerchief. "Cat, you can't keep throwing yourself from one fire into another. I love you and need to protect you."

From somewhere in her marrow, she found strength to clear away the spiders in her soul. "You're right. Jake, I need you to keep reminding me of that." She glanced around and saw Bill had disappeared. She wrapped her arms around Jake's neck. "Kiss me." He obliged.

****

Jake brightened as he saw Cat riding up to the rectory, and he joined her. The new day seemed to have swept the goblins away, seeing the lovely smile on her face. She swung down from her horse and tied the reins by the trough. "Reverend Phillips is expecting us," Jake greeted her.

He rapped on the door of the reverend's office and heard, "Come in!" They found the reverend in the midst of sorting out candy for the children's Christmas favors. He rose and shook Jake's hand. "Mr. Spencer, Miss Monroe, please have a seat." He waved toward two caned chairs that faced his desk. "Before we go on, Miss Monroe, I want to apologize for listening to the gossip about you and the late Mr. Henderson. I know now you didn't have anything to do with the deception."

Cat bowed her head. "Thank you, Reverend."

"Now, Mr. Spencer, you say you want to marry Miss Monroe?"

Jake grinned. "Yes, sir. It will be at Miss Monroe's house."

Phillips extracted a form from his desk drawer. "I'll need three weeks to post the banns. How about the second Saturday in January? What time?"

Jake and Cat exchanged a glance. "Four o'clock in the afternoon?" he asked.

Cat nodded. "With a supper to follow."

Phillips duly noted. "Mr. Spencer, would you take this to the newspaper office with you? That will save me a trip."

Jake stashed the folded form in his coat pocket. "I will, Reverend. Thank you."

All three rose and the reverend shook Jake's hand again. "Congratulations to both of you. And may God bless you."

They left the rectory, and Cat undid the reins. "I want to go to Edna's house, since you're going to the office."

He kissed her. "Meet me at the restaurant at noon." They checked their watches to see if they had the same time, then parted. Jake was happier than he had been in a long time.

****

Cat knocked on the door of the little white clapboard house. "Just a minute!" was heard from inside.

The door opened, and Edna stood there in her housedress, wiping her hands on a kitchen towel. "Cat! How good it is to see you! Come in."

Cat stepped into a small parlor with a kitchen on the other side of a cotton fabric curtain. It was pulled back, and she could see Edna had been making bread. She assumed the bedroom was behind a closed door in the back. "You're busy. Maybe I should come some other time."

"Nonsense. I just put the dough into the warming oven to rise. Sit on the couch and let me clean my hands, and then I'll bring some tea."

Cat sat on a patched but clean couch and looked around. The little house was airy, with homemade curtains on the windows. Most of the furniture was old and worn, and braided rugs covered the floors here and there. There were a few framed calendar pictures on the walls and a vase of fresh flowers on the table.

Edna brought in two cups and saucers of tea and set them down on a side table next to Cat before pulling up one of the wooden chairs for herself. "What brings you into town?"

"Jake and I are getting married."

Edna smiled and grasped her hand. "I'm so happy for you! When?"

"The second Saturday in January, at my house." Cat squeezed Edna's fingers. "I want you to be my matron of honor."

"Me? What about Polly?"

Cat glanced down. "John blames me for what happened to Father. I don't think they'll even attend."

Edna shook her head. "John is as stubborn as a Virginia mule. I hope Polly can knock some sense into him."

Cat took a breath. "Could you help me make a dress? I think, with the two of us working, we can have it done before the wedding. I want to purchase a sewing machine. That will make it go faster." Cat didn't know how to ask the next question, but she tried. "Is there a way you could come to my house to work on it?"

Edna half smiled. "You're asking me if we have the means for transportation, aren't you? Don't be embarrassed. Ed has a horse at the livery stable. Since he walks to the hotel, I could take Ben out to your house."

An hour of chatting went by, and Cat said her farewell and thanks to Edna, happy that she would be seeing her again soon. She checked her watch and hurried to the restaurant, where Jake sat at a table waiting. Her heart sang when she saw him. "I hope you haven't been here long."

He grinned. "Just five minutes. How is Edna?"

"Oh, fine. She's going to help me sew the dress. Could you hire a wagon? I want to purchase a sewing machine from the general store."

"There are always some at the livery stable. I'll get one after we eat, and meet you at the store." The waiter took their order, and after their repast, they went their separate ways.

The general store was resplendent with special doodads for Christmas. After Cat had moved into her house, she'd established an account at each of the businesses in town so she wouldn't have to worry about having enough cash on hand. She arranged for one of the two treadle sewing machines in stock to be set aside for loading.

After she studied the fashion plates located at the notions and material counter, she chose two bolts of pale blue silk and some white lace trim. A half bolt of white netting lace to be used as a veil was duly ordered, as well, and ivory buttons completed the dress items.

While she was waiting for the material, lace, and netting to be measured, a fancy pocket watch with a shutter door caught her eye in the notions display. It had a railway train embossed in gold on the shutter. The clerk came over with her packages, and she pointed to the glass case. "May I see that pocket watch, please?"

The clerk handed her the watch. "It's a fine one, miss. One like the trainmen use." She fingered the craftsmanship. Cat thought about Jake's old plain pewter watch and decided then and there this one was the perfect Christmas gift for him. "Would you like that packaged?"

She shook her head. "Just add it to my bill." She opened her reticule and dropped it in. Just in time, too, because Jake came over to her.

"One of the stockmen helped me load the machine you selected into the wagon. Are you finished here?"

She shook her head. "I wanted to get an assortment of candy for gifts."

Jake took her packages and followed her to the front counter, where she chose several small boxes of assorted chocolates and a mixed bag of hard candies. He popped one of the ribbon candies into his mouth. "Let me take those, too."

She slapped his hand. "Why? So you can eat them?" She giggled. "I haven't had time to make any gifts, so I'm buying these."

They loaded the wagon with the goods, and Cat tied Sage to the back of the wagon. Jake helped her onto the seat, then climbed up on the driver's side. With a crack of the reins, the wagon rolled out of town.

She glanced at Jake. "Could you stay for a little bit? I want to write invitations to the wedding, and you can post them in town for me."

He gave her a grimace. "Turning into a fishwife already?"

She hit him on the arm. "All right. Please?"

He grabbed her hand and kissed it. "I'm here but to serve." They laughed.

When they arrived at the house, Cat took her packages inside while Jake took Sage to the barn to bed her down. Cat put her purchases and reticule on the hall table, then hurried to the office and took out her stationery, pen, and ink.

A few minutes later Jake stepped in. "I've got Toby with me. Where do you want the machine?"

She pointed upstairs. "I'd like it in the solarium room in the turret." She paused. "Please?"

He chuckled. "You're too used to ordering around servants." He kissed her on her forehead, which made her warm. "Got to break you of that."

She finished up the invitations as she heard the heavy machine being coaxed up the stairs. Footsteps overhead told her they had made it to the solarium. She sealed the final envelope and dropped the bundle of invitations on the calling card table. Hurrying to the second floor, Cat got there just in time to see Toby leave and Jake unpinning the wooden drawers.

He glanced up and grinned. "I hope this is all right for you, because I'm not moving it another inch."

She put her fingers of her right hand to her lips and went, "Hmm."

"Catherine," he said tightly.

Then she laughed. "It's fine where it is. Thank you." She gave him a little curtsy.

Jake reached out and grabbed her around the waist, pulling her to him in an embrace. She gave a little whimper which was silenced as he clamped his mouth on hers and her body came alive like pulling a throttle on a locomotive. He broke the kiss, and she gaped at him senselessly, gulping.

He sat her down on the chaise and flipped the door closed. Her fingernails scratched at the velvet upholstery. All her brain was aware of was the memory of his body on hers and how she craved it like a fallen woman. Jake traced her curves with his hands and she vibrated like a tuning fork. He leaned in close to her ear. "I have to have you again."

Her fingers loosened the buttons of her shirtwaist and pulled it from the waist of her riding skirt. Undoing the buttons on the side of the skirt, she shimmied it to the floor. Jake had shed most of his clothes by then and freed her from the corset. Her nipples tightened when the air hit them, and she moaned as Jake caressed her breasts. They wrapped around each other, and she found intensity in the flesh on flesh. They joined, flying on wings of ecstasy, climbing the slopes to release.

Several beads of sweat wound their way down her forehead as she lay trapped in his arms for untold moments. He pulled back and chill replaced warmth. She sucked in several deep breaths. The corners of her mouth curled up. "It gets better every time."

He grinned as he pulled his clothes together. "You have the soul of a fallen woman." At her pout, he fingered her chin. "Just as long as it's with me." He kissed her.

She hurried to get herself hooked and buttoned up, stopping into her bedroom to smooth her hair. Jake was getting ready to go when she came downstairs. She handed him the invitations. "Christmas Eve is tomorrow. Remember to be here in the evening for dinner. I've invited your family, Daniel, and Ed and Edna. I knew John wouldn't accept, but I sent an invitation anyway. I hope things will change."

He embraced her. "I'll be here, of course." He pulled back. "Don't worry about John. I want you happy."

She hugged him. "Oh, I am, I am!" For the first time in several weeks, she truly was.

Chapter 25

Jake set the beautiful embossed pocket watch to the correct time under the yellow glow of all the candles and kerosene lamps in the parlor. "The watch was a perfect choice. Thank you, my love."

She fingered her pearl choker. "So was this. It's beautiful."

The guests had left, and Jake felt like lord of the manor. He couldn't wait until he no longer had to leave his lady. "I'd better go. I'll meet you after church tomorrow."

Bill brought in Jake's long coat and hat. "Here are your things, Mr. Spencer. I'm going back to help put the dishes away in the pantry."

Jake nodded. "Thank you, Bill."

Bill left, and while Jake put on his coat and hat, Cat pulled a shawl around her shoulders. They wordlessly went to the porch and lingered in the moonlit splendor, where he clasped her hand and understood everything her eyes and heart were telling him. "Good night, my darling. I agree, I can't wait until we don't have to say goodbye."

She smiled. "Good night, Jake, and Merry Christmas." They kissed, but then she tensed up. She directed his gaze to a white fluttering paper nailed to a post. "Goodness! What is that?"

Jake removed the nail and read the paper in the

light coming from the window. "You'll be sorry. Watch your back."

Cat read it over his shoulder. "What does that mean? I don't see a signature."

Fear seeped into his stomach. "Who do you think sent it?"

She chewed on her lower lip. "There's only one person I can think of that's mad at me."

"John," they both said.

Jake squeezed her arm. "I'm staying here tonight."

She shook her head. "No. I've got the staff here. He would be a fool to try anything on Christmas Eve."

Jake still doubted, but Cat was insistent. Jake opened the front door. "Bill, will you come here, please?"

Cat shook her head. "Jake, don't tell him."

He set his jaw. "This is the only way I'm leaving."

Bill showed up at the door. "Yes, Mr. Spencer?"

"Miss Monroe received a threatening message tonight. Could you be watchful for her?"

He nodded. "My room is right by the stairs. I'm a very light sleeper."

"Thank you, Bill." The butler inclined his head and left. "Now I feel better about you. One more kiss, my love." He embraced her, feeling somewhat more at ease, but a little ache of fear was in his belly. He reluctantly departed, watching her lovely form as he rode away.

****

Cat carefully peeked around the curtains of her bedroom at the gathering people. Her maid and housekeeper, Jenny and May, were helping Edna with the final touches of her dress. Jake was leaning on the hitching post, rolling a cigarette with Harvey, who had agreed to stand up with him. Daniel was just arriving with his new lady love, Lavinia. He had volunteered to stand in for her father to give her away. She didn't think John and Polly were going to show. Callahan and Jake's family were here, as well.

She sighed and drew back. *I wish John weren't so angry with me. I miss Polly and the children, too.* She tied the ribbon on her corset cover and sat at the vanity to put the finishing touches on her hair, making sure the pins were in place.

Edna touched her shoulder. "Are you ready for the dress?"

She rose. "Yes." The three women helped her into the dress, and Cat started putting the tiny pearl buttons through the loops up the front while the others draped the skirt over the bustle. The silk was nice and light. Strange to be wearing this in the middle of January, but this wasn't the winter weather she was used to. It felt more like spring.

She sat at the vanity again and handed Edna first the pearl choker to clasp at the back of her neck and then the white netting to secure in place on her head. Picking up her violet nosegay, Cat was ready to go downstairs. May and Jenny went down to announce she was coming.

Edna grasped her hand and said, with tears in her eyes, "I feel like you are my daughter about to get married."

Cat kissed her cheek. "You have always been like a mother to me. Thank you."

They went down and waited by the front door for the wedding party to assemble on the wide porch.

Family and friends would watch from the lawn.

Daniel appeared and offered her his arm. "You look beautiful, Cat."

She squeezed his elbow. "Thank you for doing this."

He smiled. "My pleasure, little sister." He opened the door, and they stepped out with Edna behind them. Daniel handed her over to Jake.

Jake had a funny mixture of love, fear, and a look as though he was about to cry on his face. She hid a grin as Edna took her place on the other side.

Reverend Phillips led them through the wedding vows, and as Jake slipped the plain gold band on her finger, she knew she would always be one with this man.

Harvey slapped Jake on the back, saying, "Congratulations, Jake! Now you'll know what it means to be tied down." He laughed.

The corners of Jake's lips curled up. "I'm a willing prisoner."

The party stepped down to the lawn and the well-wishers who had gathered there. Bill appeared from the corner of the house. "The wedding supper is ready in the back yard."

Everyone followed to a linen-covered plank table spread with a fine feast. Hettie had outdone herself. A large beef rib roast graced the center of the table, with bowls of vegetables, fruits, and hot biscuits. On a side table was a bride's cake decorated with sugared flowers.

In the midst of the merriment, Cat heard hoofbeats pounding on the road to the drive, followed by the sound of a rifle being cocked. She gasped as she saw

John aiming a rifle right at her.

In less than a second Daniel jumped at John and hit the rifle, which exploded in a blast. Jake, at the same time, knocked Cat over and shielded her. Polly, on an exhausted horse, came around the corner of the house then and moved between John and the dinner party.

"Stop this now, John," Polly cried in a voice louder than any Cat had ever heard out of her.

John struggled with Daniel, trying to stand. "Woman! Get back home where you belong!"

"No! I've had enough of your pettiness. Enough of your blaming Cat for all the troubles around here."

He pointed an accusing finger in Cat's direction. "If it wasn't for her interference, Pa wouldn't be in the penitentiary."

She took a deep breath. "You are wrong. So wrong. Pa and Logan are responsible for all that. Didn't you hear anything Pa had to say before he went away?" With his silence, she continued, "Cat is family, and Jake is part of our family now, too. Don't create a bigger sin by harming them."

Cat gently pushed Jake back and stood up. She went slowly toward John, who still held the rifle. Jake called to her, but she shushed him. "John, drop your rifle. You and Polly can come and join us for dinner and the barn dance afterward. I forgive you everything." She held out her hand to him.

For a minute or two, all that was heard was the cawing of a crow in the distance and the nicker of a few horses. John's chest heaved a couple of times, and then he lowered his rifle to the ground. "I'm sorry, Cat."

Tears welled in her eyes as she embraced her brother. Her family was close to being healed. She turned and embraced Polly, who had dismounted. "What a brave thing you did."

"I couldn't bear to lose my sister. And I'm still shaking." Polly looked down at her riding clothes. "We're not properly dressed for a dinner and dance."

Cat grasped Polly's hand. "You're family. That's all that matters."

Noticing Peggy standing not far away, Cat beckoned her over and put the other arm around her. "I have the two best sisters in the world."

Bill set two more places at the table, and Cat led them over. The guests resumed their places and finished the meal. The only casualty was the bride's cake, which had taken the brunt of the rifle blast. Bits of cake were strewn across the lawn and onto some of the trees.

Jake shook his head. "Poor Hettie. She worked so hard on that."

Cat sighed. "She cooked so much, I'm willing to leave that for the animals and birds. If Peggy wants some to put under her pillow, she's welcome to it."

Music drifted out of the barn, which had been swept clean and the horses moved to the corral. Two of Daniel's friends played squeeze box and fiddle respectably and were very good at dance music. Everyone headed to the new barn. Hettie and Bill set a table with refreshments for the dancers.

Cat touched Hettie's shoulder. "I'm sorry about the cake. It was lovely."

Hettie shook her head. "I'm just glad it was what got shot and not you or Mr. Spencer."

Cat smiled but was pulled onto the dance floor by Jake just then as the music duo started "The Bride's Waltz." Looking into his eyes as he gazed tenderly at her, she realized how close she had come to losing him less than an hour ago. Tears coursed down her cheeks.

Jake danced to the side and raised her chin with his fingers. "Hey, now, what's this?"

She paused a moment. "I realized how close I came to losing you. Promise you'll never leave me."

He gently held her. "I'll do the best I can. No one ever knows what the future has in store for us, but as long as I have a breath in me, I'm here for you."

She snuggled against his chest. "That's all I ask."

She heard a booming voice. "Boy, you have all the time in the world to bill and coo after the party. I want a dance with my new daughter-in-law." She turned, and Jake's father was holding out his hand to her. She dried her face with her handkerchief and was whirled away to the dance floor again.

Cat danced at least once with every male there, but she saved the waltzes for Jake. Finally, with a coyote howling in the distance and an owl hooting somewhere behind the barn, the party broke up. Exhausted, the young couple waved farewell to the departing carriages and horses from the porch.

Harvey also had climbed onto his mount, but he turned to Jake before riding off. "Don't bother writing this up for Monday. I'll do it. I know I told you one time to report the stories, not be one, but I can get some good ones out of you." He laughed and was gone.

Jake put his arm around Cat. "It feels good not to have to say goodbye." She shivered against him. "You must be cold. Let's go inside."

Cat gazed into his eyes from the dim light coming through the windows. She blessed the fates who had led her to him. Her heart was so full, tears puddled in her eyes. "I'm so happy you're here and loving me."

Jake opened the door and gathered her up into his arms. "A new chapter in a new home." He carried her up the stairs and closed the bedroom door.

Chapter 26

Mid-April was already hot during the afternoon, but a morning rain had cooled it enough for Cat to work on her flowers. She coaxed the little strands of climbing roses and morning glories to the porch railing and posts. Jake had built a wisteria arbor for her that led to the front porch steps.

Sweat beaded on her forehead under her broad-brimmed gardening hat, but it was the first time in weeks she'd felt well in the morning. She sat back on her knees from pulling up some stubborn weeds and wiped her face with her handkerchief. Sounds of hoofbeats in the drive brought her to her feet. She recognized the rider. "Morning, John. What brings you here?"

He dismounted and flipped the reins over the hitching post. "Morning, Cat. Is Jake here? I need to talk to him." He pointed to the plants. "Should you be doing that?"

She shaded her eyes. "I feel fine today. Jake's in the office, working on his stories for the newspaper." She pulled off her gardening gloves and brushed off her work dress. "Come in."

Bill was at the door to take John's hat, and Cat untied the ribbon on her hat and put it on the hook by the door. John turned to her. "I want to talk to Jake about some business."

At the office, Jake stood and greeted John. "This office is cramped. Let's sit in the parlor."

Bill was waiting. "May I bring you something?"

Jake nodded. "Coffee, please."

Cat replied, "Tea for me." Bill inclined his head and left.

Jake glanced at her. "Are you staying, darling?"

"I'd like to know of any business that has to do with us." Both Jake and John glanced at her and shrugged.

Bill served them from a tray and disappeared through the door. John took a sip of coffee. "I want to discuss with you about the pastureland and herd of cattle that Henderson left to us. My hired men have already removed the fence from between the two properties. I know your hired men are taking care of the former Henderson cattle. Would it be better if I built another bunkhouse at Sugar Springs so they could move there? I could pay them."

The "No" slipped out of Cat's mouth.

A surprised look came from both men. Jake turned to her. "Cat, this is man's business."

Cat felt something crush inside. "I was running it before we were married. You said I did it very well. I'd like the hired men to stay here. It's closer to the pasture, and I need them for taking care of the outbuildings."

Jake said, gently, "I'm taking care of that now."

"Since you're working at the newspaper, I'm left to run things here. Please consider what I say."

"Sounds like a Seneca Falls talk."

She gritted her teeth. "I'm not trying to get suffrage. I know what help I need that I can't do myself."

John leaned back in his chair. "Well, *Jake*, they could stay here, but I could pay them."

"No," Cat said again. "If we pay them, they'd be more inclined to help out around here. They're used to taking care of the cattle on the south pasturelands, so there wouldn't be that much of a difference."

Jake slapped his hand on the arm of the chair. "Cat, please! You'll overexcite yourself. Although, what you say makes sense."

"Thank you, dear." She wanted badly to smirk, but she lowered her head.

John glanced from one to the other. "Well?"

With a sidelong gaze at Cat, Jake replied, "I think we'll leave things as they are. You'll get the money from the cattle, of course." Both men rose and shook hands.

John turned to go. "I need to get back home." Bill appeared with John's hat. "Thank you, Bill." He put it on. "I want to invite you to supper Friday next. I have something I want both of you to see."

Jake slapped him on the shoulder. "I'll put it on my calendar. Let me see you off."

As the two men closed the door, Cat gave a little squeak of victory. Men might think they're making the decisions, but a wise woman can influence in subtle ways, her aunt used to tell her. Well, maybe Cat wasn't so subtle, but she'd accomplished the goal. She chuckled and picked up her knitting from the basket by her chair, humming softly to herself.

****

The sun indicated at least another hour of light in the lengthening spring days as the carriage carried Jake and Cat to Sugar Springs. A surprise met them as they saw Callahan's carriage in the drive to the house.

John and Polly had moved their family into the big white house from their little cabin a couple of months ago, with Cat and Jake helping them. Sam and Aggie were playing on the lawn. "Pa! Ma! Uncle Jake and Aunt Cat are here!" hollered Sam, as he ran through the front door.

Jake helped Cat down as John came out with Sam. Sam ran and jumped into Jake's arms. "We're going out to—"

"Sam, hush!" John said, sharply. Callahan, Jake's parents, Peggy, Daniel, and Polly came out on the porch. John waved his hand. "Everyone, we're going out for a bit before supper, so get back in your carriages and on your horses."

"Can we go with Uncle Jake?" Sam piped up.

John nodded. "If that's all right with him."

Jake and Cat settled the children in the back seat of the carriage and climbed in. Others took to their own transportation and followed John and Polly toward the pasture.

The construction road toward the hills was little more than a couple of ruts through the grass. The carriages rumbled and bumped their way to the incline by the stream, where John and Polly dismounted and the rest of the party did the same or got down from their carriages.

Jake and Cat picked up Sam and Aggie respectively. Cat waved at John. "Now what?"

John pointed to a small incline which led to a large plateau, somewhat like a lookout ridge. "Everyone, go up there." John and Polly took Sam and Aggie. Jake helped Cat up the hill, and then John directed their attention to the springs, a short distance away. "I'm ready to fix the wrong that brought all this trouble in the first place. Cover your ears." He waved both his hands.

A second went by, followed by an explosion of dirt, stones, wood, and water. Everyone gasped as the brown cloud billowed up where the dam had been. Water hurtled to its natural fork and flowed evenly to the west and south.

Callahan stepped to John and shook his hand. "Thank you, my boy. That was a neighborly thing to do."

The procession filed back to the house for a feast of celebration. John rose after the dishes had been cleared away, holding a piece of paper. "As an explanation of the spectacle before dinner, I received this letter from Pa a little over a week ago. It reads:

"I've been sitting in this cell contemplating the grievous and selfish things I did to bring me here. I want you to make things right. Blow the partial dam up in a celebration for the family and neighbors. Tell them I was responsible for the whole thing, and the springs should flow as God intended them to. If I ever come home, I want to come home to peace and harmony with all. I can't bring back Logan and Ned, some things I'll have to pay for here, but let's put right what we can."

Cat closed her eyes, and a tear trickled down her cheek. Jake tenderly put his arm around her. They were all there at Sugar Springs. Cat glanced around. John and Daniel sitting together. She and Jake were accepted as family. Callahan, Jake's parents, and Peggy were at the table. Her father had brought them all together in peace and harmony, as he put it.

As they readied to leave for the evening, Cat embraced Polly on the porch. "Thank you for your part in bringing John to accept us. Was this all part of your plan?"

She smiled. "I wrote to Pa Monroe and told him what was happening here. It was his letter that drove John straight."

"That and the scene at my wedding. Polly, I was so proud of you!"

Tears welled in Polly's eyes. "I couldn't let John do that. Not to family." She embraced Cat again. "And now you're with child. Come to me if you need any help. I've done that twice."

"I will." Cat made her way down the steps to where Jake was waiting with the carriage. He helped her up and climbed in beside her.

The night was black, with only the canopy of stars above them. Jake snorted. "I can't see where we are going."

Cat laughed. "Tawny, home!" she called out to the horse. Immediately, the steed started walking down the drive. "He'll find the way."

Jake dropped the reins across his lap. "Cat, I've been thinking on what I said to you last week. About man's business. I'm sorry about that, but I just didn't want to burden you. Especially now."

"I'm sorry, too, but you have to understand if I feel strongly about something, I'm going to speak out."

He put his arm around her and drew her in close. "I know how hard you struggled when you first got the property and had to rebuild the barn. I want to make sure you don't have to go through that anymore."

She snuggled into the warmth with no end of love

for this man. The steady clip-clop of the horse was lulling her to sleep. The shaking of the carriage as it turned into the drive woke her, and she saw the yellow glow of the lights from the house windows. Bill had set one of the lanterns on the wicker porch table for them.

Jake helped Cat down. "I'll put the carriage away and bed down Tawny. Wait here for me."

She sat on the porch railing, watching the spectacular sky with its shooting stars, and instead of making a wish, she thanked her God that she had come to Arizona. She heard the crunch of boots coming through the arbor and up the steps. The breeze ruffled the wisps of her hair that refused to be pinned up.

A warm arm went around her, and she leaned into Jake's chest, listening to his heartbeat. This was the home she had been searching for. She had a family who wanted her and a husband who loved her. And soon that would be added to. She laid her hand lightly on her slightly rounded belly.

Jake leaned to her ear. "Let's go inside."

Cat picked up the lantern and gave it to Bill, who met them at the door. He took their wraps and Jake's hat. "All is well, Mr. Spencer."

"Everything?"

Bill gave a slight nod. "Yes, sir."

Cat frowned as Bill left. "What was that all about?"

Jake laughed. "You'll see." He grasped her hand and they hurried upstairs. Just outside their bedroom door, he stopped her. "Wait out here until I tell you to come in." He lit the lamp. "Now."

She came in and noticed something by the bed. She knelt down and found a beautiful mahogany cradle. She ran her hand along the smooth wood. "Oh, it's lovely!

Is this what you were doing out in the barn?"

"Yes, darling. Do you like it?"

In answer, she rose and kissed him thoroughly. Here she would stay.

A word about the author...

Ilona Fridl works over her computer in a lovely city in SE Wisconsin. She's been married to Mark for over forty years. She credits her success to Kathie Giorgio of AllWriters for giving her wings to soar. Her family is getting smaller but is still very dear.

Web site: http://www.ilonafridl.com

www.ingramcontent.com/pod-product-compliance
Lightning Source LLC
Chambersburg PA
CBHW070334260626
47160CB00003B/1043